THE MICHELLE–
SURFACE'S
END

DAVID JOEL STEVENSON

THANKS!!

Printed in the United States of America

First Printing, 2015
Edited, 2016

ISBN-13: 978-1517772888
ISBN-10: 1517772885

www.DavidJoelStevenson.com

Cover Design: Michael Hutzel, Fox Fuel Creative
Cover Photo: Mykola Mazuryk, Shutterstock

CHAPTER ONE

Never go near the Deathlands.

This was a rule that everyone in the village could agree on. When a child asked his parents the inevitable question, "Why?," a seriousness would wash over their faces. The answers would often sound like ghost stories; tales to strike fear into the hearts of would-be adventurers. The children, when left alone, would trade theories, letting their imaginations get the best of them. They would talk about their plans to discover the mystery of the Deathlands.

But when the time for action was presented, their bravery waned.

Jonah Whitfield sat at the top of a lonely hill overlooking the desolate wasteland. *It's not that bad*, he thought to himself.

Just depressing, really.

He finished off the bread that was in his satchel, brushing the crumbs off his shirt. Lingering for only a moment, he gathered his things and stood, turning his back away from the cracked plain toward the green direction of home. His hunt had been only somewhat successful, but he knew that in order to get to the village by dark, he had to get moving.

Placing his weapons on top of the rabbit carcasses strapped to his bicycle's makeshift trailer, he jumped on the seat and started coasting down the grassy slope. He picked up as much speed as he could on the uneven ground, closing his blue eyes as the wind blew into his face and shaggy brown hair.

He was thankful for the mostly wooden bike – he and his father had put a lot of work into resurrecting it from trashed chains and gears. Without it, it would be impossible to travel the distance from here to town in less than a day unless he rode on horseback. He never liked the idea of keeping one of the family's horses away from the farm for any time.

Unlike the obvious barren expanse behind, the landscape in front of him was lush, alive, and painted with color. The change between the two was abrupt, like someone dug up the wilderness and replaced it with useless, clumped dust. It looked as if a snake shed its skin, but in this case it was reversed – the live fell away and the dead remained.

Some people said it was similar to deserts they'd heard about in the rest of the country.

"It's just a lack of rain," they'd say. "It's normal."

But there was an understanding that it was not normal. Jonah had seen the sterile land soaked in the same storms as the grass mere inches away on multiple occasions.

Jonah frequently hunted near the edge of the Deathlands, hanging around not out of rebellion as much as out of curiosity. It was a prime location since none of the other towns folk came this direction in search of wild game, so the animals weren't as thinned out — at least not as much as just about everywhere else he'd seen. He'd been coming for almost two years now, starting just after his fifteenth birthday, when his father decided it was officially time to pass the torch. It was up to Jonah to provide the bulk of the meat for his five member family, and he found it to be a welcomed responsibility.

When he first established this hunting location, it seemed that the Deathlands were a great distance away. Over the last two years, either because of his physical growth or because of his familiarity with the desolation, it seemed to inch toward him.

In recent months, the animals weren't quite as numerous. He was the only one hunting there to his knowledge, and didn't think it was possible that he had thinned them out himself. He assumed it was only temporary, but lately he was starting to wonder if something else was scaring them away.

.- .-- .- -.- .

After dusk had descended, a few hours after he started his journey, he pedaled his bike between log homes with candlelight shining through the foggy glass windows. The houses were in the midst of fields, fenced in animals, and patches of trees trickling in from the forest behind.

Jonah slowed his pace to wave at the occasional neighbor who was finishing up chores, or child who would run toward him with hopes of him stopping to play. He smiled at the simple routine, glancing up at the first stars of the evening. Usually the expanse of the sky made him feel tiny, but on some occasions he simply felt like it was only there to be the backdrop of the sleepy town.

When he saw the lights from his home in the distance, he subconsciously picked up speed.

After jumping off his bike and catching his breath, he pumped a few gallons of water out of the well into a large basin. He carried the carcasses into the shed that was readied to clean and butcher his kill – whatever it might be. He removed his jacket and washed what remained of the animals' dried blood off his hands, then crossed the yard to the back of the log cabin that was his home. As he opened the squeaky door, he saw his mother, Helen, turn while wiping her hands on her apron. Her red hair was dusted with flour.

"Just in time," she smiled. "Looks like you had a good trip."

"It was okay," he said as he slipped into his chair at the dinner table, his legs tired from the day's travel. "Maybe ten pounds worth of meat after I get done cleaning them."

"That will get us through the week, but the ice box is getting pretty low. You're getting harder to keep fed these days, you know!" She chuckled as she brought a bowl of mashed potatoes to the table, calling out, "Dinner's ready!"

Jonah smiled and rolled his eyes a bit. At just under six feet tall, it was plain that his height had reached its peak, but his mother still talked about her 'growing baby.' Secretly, he appreciated the obvious affection, but was embarrassed when she used such language around the other town folk - especially within earshot of the girls his age.

He leaned over the table and drew in a large breath through his nose. Fried chicken, though a common meal since their chicken coop was a consistent provider of meat, always hit the spot. "I left a few traps set up," he continued, "so I'm planning on going back out in a couple of days. I haven't seen them, but I'm positive that the deer are still there," he said, hoping aloud.

"Might be time to find a new spot," she answered. "Seems like you're bringing back less and less each time you're out there."

"Yeah..."

He knew she was right, but felt a tinge of sadness knowing that his routine might be changed. It would be different if the change was because of something... adventurous... But since it was merely to find a new place to do the same thing he was already doing, it felt like he was retreating. Gazing out into the Deathlands at least felt a *bit* exciting, just knowing he was on the boundary of commonplace.

His younger brother and sister, Harrison and Lillian, bounded in the room giggling to each other. At eleven and thirteen, respectively, they were still mostly able to remain children and avoided most of the 'responsibility' talks over the past couple of years.

Jonah's father slowly limped through the living room door into the kitchen, his right hand clenching his walking cane. He eased into the chair at the end of the table and took the glass of water that Harrison held out to him. "Thanks bud," he said as Helen bent down and kissed him on the cheek. She placed a plate of cornbread on the table near him. "How was the hunt, Jonah?"

"Maybe ten pounds of rabbit... I'm planning on going back out in a couple of days."

"That's my boy," his father responded proudly. "Determined to do what he needs to feed this family. If it wasn't for this... *this*—" His voice rose slightly.

Helen looked at him, a single eyebrow raised as if to say *watch which word you choose.*

"This *aggravating* leg," he concluded, forgetting that he was in the middle of a sentence. He let out a deep sigh.

"We're lucky it was just the leg, Tom," Helen reminded him.

Thomas Whitfield sat awkwardly silently for a moment, his eyes staring down at the limb that seemed to hold him down. Jonah had no doubt that his father's mind was on the accident that took his mobility from him almost two years ago.

As Helen sat down next to him, Thomas bowed his head further, and the rest of the Whitfields followed suit. "Lord, we thank You for this food that You've provided for us. Help us not to concentrate on what we don't have, but on the many blessings that You've given us. Amen."

"Amen," the family repeated.

Jonah glanced at his father, and saw that his eyes watered

slightly.

After recovering from the accident, Thomas had reluctantly taken Jonah aside to tell him that he was counting on him – that the whole family was counting on him – to take up the slack. The injured man wept bitterly, thinking he had let everyone down. Since then, he'd been determined to do everything he could, from butchering Jonah's kills to tending their large garden alongside Helen, albeit much slower than she.

But he still felt like an unnecessary weight.

"You know, I've been thinking," Jonah said, trying to break up his father's obviously frustrating train of thought. "I could fix up that trailer that I use for my bike, and you could sit in it – maybe even figure out some way to help pedal. Then we could go hunting together... You can shoot, you know. It's just getting out there that's preventing it right now."

A smile came across Thomas's face. "That'd be great, bud," he said as a happier tear slid out of the corner of his eye before he could catch it with his handkerchief. His tone picked up slightly, "but you've got enough on your shoulders right now. No sense in adding to your workload."

"No trouble. Maybe Harrison could help?" He looked over at his brother, whose mouth was full of potatoes, nodding. "It might take a while, but I know we can do it."

Though Thomas was obviously appreciative, he changed the subject. Dinner continued as it did most nights, listening to stories from everyone's day.

.- .-- .- -.- .

Jonah was jarred awake by the rooster crowing just outside his window.

The sun was still far from the horizon, but he sat up, stretching and yawning silently. He looked outside, wondering if the rooster was simply there to wake him, or if it thought that its crow would actually bring the dawn.

I guess now is as good a time as any, he thought to himself, tossing the blankets off his legs. Harrison stirred in the nearby bed, but resumed a slight snore only moments later. With all three children sharing the same bedroom, and a rooster that found apparent joy in dispersing early morning dreams, Jonah's younger siblings had learned to sleep fairly heavily. Jonah, however, never allowed himself to sleep through much of anything. If he ever nodded off while waiting for prey, he didn't want his dreams to interfere with the reason he was patiently still.

It only happened once. He had found the perfect climbing tree, rested his gun on a branch, and leaned against the trunk. He had prepared to be gone for up to three days, and this was but an hour into the first day's hunt. After taking a sip of water from his canteen he closed his eyes, concentrating on the noises around him. The breeze blowing through the leaves, the lonely owl hooting across the woods, the sound of an animal rummaging through his food...

His eyes had jumped open quickly, seeing the hind end of a wild boar disappear into nearby brush. He tried to pull the gun up to his shoulder, but it was on the ground below him, next to his opened satchel. The time to shoot had long past, the sun was high and everything was exposed by its light, revealing that the animal had retreated well before he was even aware. His gaze fell downward, seeing his three-day-supply of food gone. He had never returned the top to his canteen, and the water had soaked through what little crumbs remained. He was so angry at himself that he decided to immediately return home, knowing that he would not have been focused enough to hunt for the day – and he no longer had the food to stay out longer.

Never again, he had said.

This morning, only a couple of days since he had returned from his last hunt, he quietly moved into the kitchen to the back door. Throwing a jacket on over his clothes, he quickly shoved some cornbread in his mouth and slipped an apple in his pocket for the bike ride. He grabbed his satchel, which was full of leftovers that his mother packed him. His sister had sewn a strap to his rifle not long after the failed hunt, so it could not fall out of reach if he again got too comfortable. Though he vowed it wouldn't happen again, he agreed that it was a good addition.

Once inside the shed he grabbed his flintlock muzzleloader rifle and bow, the tools of his trade. Luckily, before the animals were thinning, he stocked up on the round bullets and gunpowder he needed from his extra kills. Ammunition might as well have been currency in the sprawling farm town, so the town blacksmith didn't have as much to worry about in terms of where his meals would come from.

Jonah dropped a bag of bullets in his satchel, and grabbed a quiver of arrows as a last resort. He was a good enough shot with his rifle, but it would take too long to reload if he merely wounded his target. He never liked to leave home unprepared, and an arrow was much easier to prepare in a pinch.

Placing all of his gear into the empty bicycle trailer, he threw his leg over and pushed off into the still coal black morning. He had traveled the path so often that he barely even needed the wisp of moonlight that reflected the fresh dew. The air was silent except for his tires against the long grass, and methodical squeak from the bike chain.

Need to put some oil on that, he thought to himself. *That could give me away for miles.*

He had set out even earlier than he realized, because a few hours later, when he arrived at his tree near the Deathlands, the sun still had not peaked over the horizon.

He strapped on his satchel and canteen, then wheeled the bike under a nearby fallen limb. He paused after climbing the tree, taking a brief moment to admire his surroundings. As he did every hunt, he said a quick prayer, asking that his effort would provide food for his family and friends. He hid himself in the twigs and leaves so that he would still be inconspicuous when the darkness had disappeared. He rested his gun on the branch, loaded it with powder, wadding, and a bullet, then closed his eyes to listen to the sounds of the morning.

Hours later, he had heard nothing more than a few birds and a tiny rodent in a nearby bush. The sun was prominently hanging in the sky, and all the dew from the morning had disappeared. He considered removing his jacket since the heat would most likely only increase, but he was always wary of too much movement. He could cancel out the effort of his stillness in the preceding morning with the simple action. As such, he refrained.

Jonah took a quick, silent drink from his canteen, which he had placed on a branch close to his face. As soon as his right hand slid back to the trigger, he saw the bushes at the edge of the woods rustle. Judging by the movement, whatever caused it was large. This was no rodent.

Jonah froze.

The bushes were too far to his left to easily train his gun without making a bit of a commotion through the tree limbs, so he waited. If it was something worth shooting he would make his movement, but there was no sense in drawing attention to himself if not. He turned his head to see what was making the noise, but continued to wait, unable to decipher if he saw antlers or simply branches swaying with the motion of the brush.

He sat for what seemed like another hour in the uncomfortable position; his head elevated and chin an inch away from his left shoulder, while the rest of his body pointed forward. More than once he thought about giving up, assuming he would have at least confirmed by that point that his target was something he'd like to eat. But hearing the words of his father echo in his head, *"Determined to do what he needs to to feed his family,"* he decided he could take the discomfort. Knowing what his father would give to be in this tree, with this freedom of motion, he felt that he couldn't give up. He didn't know if this would be the only time this trip that he'd have an opportunity for big game – if indeed it was big game – because it had been so long since he'd seen any around here.

In an instant, a huge buck waltzed out of the brush as if he owned the ground it walked on. His antlers were covered with points – more than Jonah had ever seen before. It looked around, first toward the direction of Jonah's home, and then towards the Deathlands.

If he walks towards town, Jonah thought, *there's no way I can get him. By the time I get my gun on him, he'll be deep in the woods again.* He continued to wait.

As if it saw Jonah and wanted to make his acquaintance, it started walking straight towards the tree. Jonah held his breath. As the buck neared the tree, it turned left toward the Deathlands, slowly walking in a straight line.

Jonah kept his eyes locked on the animal, but was helpless. The graceful deer was far too close, and the branch he used to rest his gun prohibited him from pointing downward. He couldn't move, because it would definitely hear him from that distance. The buck idly nibbled on fallen nuts, oblivious to the thoughts of the predator above him.

Keep going, Jonah urged in his mind. *Keep going.*

As if the deer knew what Jonah wanted, it slowly walked forward about fifteen paces, giving him enough range of motion to aim – though the shot would most likely not kill the animal before it had time to run far enough away from Jonah to lose it. He held the rifle tight to his shoulder, and squinted his eyes with the buck in his sights. He knew that he would most likely have only an instant if the animal decided to run.

As if God Himself had placed this animal in front of Jonah,

the deer turned broadside.

The scenario that was made available could not be better. He squeezed the trigger.

As soon as the bullet left the chamber, he knew it would find the animal's heart. The buck took off running, but ran completely opposite of where Jonah assumed it would.

It ran *toward* the Deathlands as fast as it could.

Jonah had never seen an animal in the Deathlands, as he assumed that they were all as afraid of it as the townspeople were.   There was nothing that drew them into it; no nourishment or shelter existed in the naked expanse. But in this instance, nothing was drawing the animal into the desolation – it was simply fleeing from where the bullet originated, with no thought as to where it would go. Just away.

Jonah let out the air that he had stored in his lungs, pausing a moment to celebrate his assumed kill. The buck ran hard in a straight line, slowing down in the distance, but still with strength in its muscles. Blood dripped on the pale ground, as if glowing in contrast. It ran so hard that it was soon out of sight, which gave Jonah a surprise.

I have to go into the Deathlands to retrieve it.

Though he had spent so much time looking into the wasteland, he'd never dared step foot in it. And he'd never had the intention of traveling so deep into it that he would not be seen from the edge. He somberly gathered himself and his belongings and eased down the tree.

He stared across the expanse as if the deer was gone forever, never to be found. But he saw the trail of blood leading into the heart of the sterile landscape, and knew that he could not give up.

As he walked to the edge, where the green stopped and the gray began, he recalled some of the tales that his childhood friends had swapped.

"I heard that if you touch the Deathlands, your whole body shrivels up."

"Well, I heard that somebody got close to it, and his brother died at the exact same time!"

"I know somebody that saw the Deathlands swallow up a horse, like it's just a huge mouth."

Ghost stories, he reasoned. *Just tales to keep kids away. They only want to make sure no one gets lost.*

Walking very far into the Deathlands would surely disorient anyone. No landmarks, no indication of direction. He couldn't count on following the trail of blood back out once he went in, because it could easily seep into the ground, or a rain storm could come while he was out there and wash it away.

After looking around, he decided on a way to lead him back out of the expanse; he would wrap pieces of his orange sleeves around limbs that he would stick into the ground. He gathered sturdy branches, took off his jacket, and ripped his sleeves off in strips. His mother had dyed the shirt with carrot juice, and he hoped it would stand out against the pale gray ground.

He tossed the homemade flags into the trailer, and walked the bike to the edge, sticking the first flag in the grass just outside of the edge.

Just stupid ghost stories, he pleaded with himself, almost expecting the flag to be consumed by the dirt. He looked behind him, as if his parents were watching, shaking their fingers in disapproval.

He took his first step onto the undiscovered land.

And nothing happened.

He wheeled the bike and trailer onto the gray ground cautiously.   Gazing around him preparing for some unseen danger, his mind was continually trying to decipher the sounds coming into his ears.   Birds in the distance sounded like warnings, the wind against his face like screams.

Slowly, he followed the spattering of blood, sticking flags into the ground as he walked.   The flags did not go in easily – it was as if the ground was solid, not like rock, but not simply dirt.   He hammered them in with the butt of his gun.

Gaining confidence with each step, he picked up speed, and eventually hopped onto the seat of his bike, constantly looking back to make sure he was always within sight of the last flag.   He placed fifteen flags before he saw the deer in the distance.

How in the world did it survive this far? he wondered.

He returned thanks, remembering his prayer before the hunt – thinking especially of the perfect shot he had.

He slowed down, slid off the seat, and wheeled his bike toward the carcass.

About two feet before he reached the lifeless animal, his trailer ran upon something large and solid.   Intrigued, as the rest of the land had been eerily smooth, he wheeled the bike out of the way and inspected the ground.

It was a mound of dirt – or whatever the substance making up the ground was – that rose about three inches above the rest of the surface. He leaned down, and ran his hand over the mound, for a brief moment looking up to again confirm that no one – and no*thing* – was watching.

Why am I so paranoid? There's nobody for miles... And if the Deathlands were... cursed... I would've already seen or felt something.

He started to dig away at the mound, and to his surprise, soon found a piece of rusted metal. He continued to dig, at first simply moving loose dirt. However, in not too much time he had to use the remaining limbs from unused flags in place of a shovel.

The emerging object was a large wheel, about the width of his forearm. Six spokes led towards the middle, still submerged in the ground.

I've seen one of these before... At the junkyard. What could it be doing out here?

He continued to remove the dirt from the wheel, expecting it to come free from the ground. He would take it to John Schultz, and perhaps even get something in return for it. All the scrap metal he'd ever seen was at Schultz's junkyard, and he couldn't think of anything else he could do with it – but he didn't want to just leave it out here. He tugged on it from both sides, his sleeveless muscles tensing, but it didn't seem to give.

He took a limb and struck the dirt near the middle of the ring of metal, where it seemed to converge, assuming that it was merely more solid ground that held it there.

As he dug, he found that the wheel was attached to something - something bigger - and he couldn't help but continue unearthing what he found.

After he had been at it for some time, he had uncovered a surface wider than the wheel itself. Knowing that it might take far too long to dig the entire thing out of the ground, seemingly impossible actually, he started to simply rub the sandy gray dust off what he had already exposed. He started near the base of the original metal ring. As he rubbed he recognized that it was more metal, but it curiously had no rust. In fact, it was perfectly polished.

He had never seen perfectly polished metal. Everything he had seen, even the new creations from the blacksmith, were dented and rough. Gun barrels, even meticulously maintained, had grown dull. Whoever placed this in the ground obviously spent a long time with every inch of its surface area – or had built some fantastic machine to polish it for them. And to find metal that had been exposed to the elements without rust was very strange.

Continuing to clean the surface, he uncovered a curious patch of colors. Jonah had never seen such precision. A perfect rectangle, seemingly *in* the metal, with alternating stripes of red and white. In the top left corner of the rectangle was a smaller rectangle of blue with a large number of perfect white stars spaced inside equally.

And below the image, chiseled in tiny immaculate text, were three simple words.

MADE IN CHINA

CHAPTER TWO

Jonah woke up early, removed the quilt from his body and returned it to the trailer where he had unpacked it the evening before. It was just after dawn, and a slight chill was still in the air. He used coals to relight the fire that he built the previous night and huddled close.

He thought about yesterday, wondering if it had been a dream. Noting that he just saw the large buck in the trailer when he returned the quilt, he knew that it was no dream.

Yesterday, after digging even more, then staring at the extensive amount of polished metal for longer than he knew, he realized there was nothing he could do at the moment. He had a dead deer next to him, and multiple traps still set from the previous expedition. He could have tried to continue to dig, but he didn't know when he would completely lose daylight. He definitely didn't want to try to navigate with the flags in the darkness.

He had loaded the deer into the trailer and placed a final flag. Not that he'd need the flag to see the gigantic hole in the ground in the middle of a gray canvas, but he had figured the precaution couldn't hurt.

When he had turned to leave, he surveyed his surroundings. He knew that the Deathlands went on beyond what his vision could take in when standing on the edge, but when in the middle of it... It was overwhelming. In the distance was the fifteenth flag, and the fourteenth was nowhere to be seen. He couldn't see anything in any direction. For a moment, he naïvely thought that he must be in the center of this desert, but then realized he had no idea just how much farther in the center might be.

Perhaps he could walk, placing another fifteen, thirty, even a hundred flags and not reach the other side. For all he knew, there was no other side... He always assumed that the Deathlands was like a pond in the middle of the land. But the thought crossed his mind that it could be the other way around – the town might be the island in the middle of a desolate ocean.

He had learned in school that the earth was round, and man had once explored the entire planet in search of new places in ships as large as their town. He knew that there came a point when nothing was left to explore – no new lands to discover. He had also heard stories that something terrible had occurred, generations in the past, which caused countless communities to disappear and numerous lives to end.

However, he knew no one that traveled further than a town or two away. What if the great disaster was that these oceans that he had heard of became the Deathlands? What if the undrinkable water had dried up, and all the life sustained by them ceased?

After shaking his head, as if to force the thoughts out, he had pedaled his bike towards the flags, towards the edge of the bare ground, towards life as he'd always known it. However – a massive piece of underground metal with perfect colors and letters in a place that was completely off limits to everyone that he knew...

That didn't fit into life as he'd always known it.

Obvious questions about the object arose. *How did it get there? Why is it still there? How has nothing unearthed it before now? How are the metal, letters, and colors so perfect and uniform?*

His first thought in trying to answer the questions were to find the similar scrap wheel that he knew he'd seen at Schultz's... Maybe he'd even know what China was, or why it would be etched into the surface he'd discovered.

When he crossed the threshold back to grass, he had quickly switched to task mode. He field dressed the deer and went around to check his traps – two squirrels and another rabbit. Not bad for so little effort, *but not great, either,* he thought. After washing himself in a stream that was just beyond the brush where he first saw the buck, he returned to his preferred hill. He had started a fire, filled his belly, and fallen asleep.

Currently, while warming breakfast over the fire, he was wondering what to do.

If he went home now, which is what he would normally do after a successful kill of this size, he would be hard pressed to find a reason to return for a few days without raising suspicion. With a large supply of meat that would last the Whitfields for well over a month, he would have no reason to return to hunt. And since only a couple of days ago he had basically insisted that his father come with him on a future trip, riding in the trailer, he couldn't simply reject him from tagging along if he waited to return until his family was again running low on meat. Especially since he'd have enough time over the next month to modify the trailer the way he had talked about with his father.

I could leave the deer, he briefly thought, *but that would be a terrible waste of good meat.*

Considering how little big game he had seen for the past few months, *it would be downright stupid*, he reasoned, shaking his head at even having the thought. The buck lying in his trailer might very well be the last deer that he would see in this area. Returning empty handed would feel bad enough without knowing that there would be a rotting carcass where he was standing now.

He thought about butchering the deer there on the trailer and stocking it into the ice box and smokehouse without anyone knowing. That would definitely be better than wasting the deer, no question.

The problems he faced would be in how he would actually do it, though. He knew that if anyone saw him while he was riding up or loading it, he would be found out. Besides, what would his mother say when there was an ice box magically full of venison – a place that she frequented at least every other day?

Another unusable idea.

Jonah stared out over the barren land, slowly chewing the leftovers from the previous dinner as morning vittles, with his curiosity burning inside him. He had no idea what the metal piece was, but he felt the need - the compulsion - to find out.

He couldn't let anyone know that not only had he set foot on the Deathlands, but that he also dug up a mysterious object inside it. Either they'd never let him leave because of the rules and stories, or he would not be able to keep the gawkers away.

In both cases, he would lose the secret that he felt he owned at this moment.

He searched for ways to convince his family that he needed to come back to this place, without raising suspicion. Something that would draw him to his normal sanctuary, but with no expectation of bringing anything back beyond what he took with him. Some reason for stuffing his satchel full of supplies, and no questions of why.

What, besides wild game, could bring me back here? he wondered, his lips moving as if the motion would spur on a conversation. *Some other resource or necessity...*

He jerked as the idea started forming in his head.

He could create the need. He could leave something here - something important - so that it would be obvious that he should come back. Instead of planning on returning from his *next* trip without meat, he could return with less now.

But what could he leave?

He couldn't leave something as crucial as his gun or bow. He would never be that irresponsible – his family knew that, so it would most likely raise suspicion. On top of that, he couldn't risk actually losing either, or allow them to sit in the dew or rain.

Nor could he leave something as commonplace as his knife, fashioned from animal bone and a piece of metal from Schultz's wares. His father would be quick to make a new one, anxious for the contribution he could make.

Glancing over his belongings, the decision seemed simple enough; he would leave his satchel.

It contained a handful of things that might be seen as unacceptable to lose – namely his stock of bullets. Considering that, and the fact that the small bag was fashioned by his mother out of the hide of the first deer he had killed, he assumed the return for it would raise no questions.

Realizing that he knew a way to buy time, he hesitated. He squinted his blue eyes in the direction of his questions. It did not make sense to waste these hours. If he returned now, he would merely get home early to daydream about where he was at this exact moment. It was early, and no one expected him home until the next day. He didn't like the idea of letting the meat from the hunt the day before sit overnight, so he decided he'd return tonight – but he could still explore.

Jonah mounted his bicycle, and again trekked toward the object. After his sleep, he had forgotten the length of the distance that he crossed before, still following blood stains on the ground and the protruding flags. He kept the time in mind, knowing that he had a long ride back home, this time with the extra weight of the meat in the back. He realized it might have been a good idea to have left the trailer by the tree, but it was too late to consider it now. He continued to pedal.

He arrived at the object, unchanged from the previous day. It seemed as if even the wind was afraid of stirring the dust that he had disturbed.

He studied the gleaming surface while pacing around it, as if it were a coiling snake. After circling for an extended period, he approached with hesitation and even a bit of grace – as if the object had to be charmed for it to answer his questions.

He resumed unearthing the area surrounding the wheel. As if someone had placed his greatest treasure a few feet below the surface, he put his questions into the form of the labor of his dig; quickly, but careful not to harm what was below the dirt.

Over the next few hours, he uncovered a slightly rounded raised edge, forming a perfect circle hovering six inches below the wheel. Below the edge, the metal continued straight down for at least the length of the tips of his fingers to his wrists. The width of the circle was about the same size as the family's well opening – roughly the size needed for a man to move around inside.

Is there something below this surface that could be drawn up like water?

He knew it could not be water that would be drawn up... Any water that might have pooled below the surface would have at least caused seedlings of grass to spring up. But regardless of what would come out of the object, the thought occurred to him that he was staring at a sealed hole. Much in the same way his own well was covered by wood and stone, this hole might be enclosed to keep away the elements and animals.

Perhaps the purpose of its seal was not to keep something out of it, he wondered, but rather keep something *in* it. And that the thing inside of it – if that was the case – was killing the land. But much like the legend of the box given to Pandora, that thought was quickly suppressed by the weight of his curiosity.

He tugged on the wheel, hoping that by loosening the ground from around the edge he would have released its hold.

Still nothing.

He took one of the largest limbs from in his trailer, inserting it below the wheel spokes and rested one end on the ground. He crouched as low to the ground as he could, and placed the other end of the limb on his shoulder. Creating as much leverage as possible, he began to stand up, staring at the wheel with bulging eyes. Harder.

He growled from deep in his throat and pushed with every ounce of strength in his body. Harder.

He felt that he could hear the strain of his muscles squeaking in the wood on his shoulder. *Harder.*

CRACK!

The limb in his hands broke and he stumbled forward, tripping over the object that was seemingly unmovable.

He had lost track of time – digging, pausing to let his mind wander, and digging again, often repeating those steps – and he felt that he might need to gather as much information as possible and simply return later.

Schultz would be a strong ally – he knew more about what

he called *machinery* than anyone else in town, and it looked like this could be some of that.

Loading everything into his cart, he straddled his bicycle and slowly moved away from the object. He checked each flag as he passed them, confirming that they were deep enough to keep their position in wind or rain.

After he crossed the threshold of the Deathlands, he hid his satchel in a knot in his tree.

.- .-- .- -.- .

Jonah finished his breakfast before his father even reached the kitchen table.

"Hold your horses, bud! This food isn't going anywhere," Thomas smirked.

Jonah wiped the crumbs from his mouth. "I know – I... I'd like to get to Schultz's early to see what kind of materials I could use to make some new traps." He cleared his throat a bit.

"You know, you just brought home enough meat to last us at least a month – you could take a break for a day or two," his mother said softly.

"I will," he quickly responded, obviously not registering what the words actually meant. "I'll just rest a bit easier if all the traps are covered. Besides – if I have to go back for *only* the satchel, I'll feel like I've wasted a trip out there."

Helen shook her head. "It just isn't like you to leave your

things out there like that. You're usually so careful."

His family had hesitantly bought his story about being so preoccupied with getting the buck prepared for the trip back that he 'must have left the satchel on the ground.' They weren't quite so convinced, however, when he tried to explain why his shirt sleeves were missing.

He hadn't quite prepared himself for that question, so he stumbled through it a bit. He finally arrived at telling them that he ripped off the sleeves to use them as rags to clean himself up after field dressing the deer. "Why didn't you bring them back to wash?" his mother had asked with curious eyes. "You didn't just throw them on the ground, did you?"

He played the part of absent minded – which wasn't completely untrue in regards to that question. Nothing went to waste in the Whitfield house or the entire town. Table scraps went to the animals, old wood went in the stove, worn out clothing became patches for other clothing that was nearing the same fate. Anything else ended up at Schultz's, to eventually be used by someone else.

Once leaving his house, after an awkward breakfast and a quick bicycle ride, he pedaled between the junkyard piles looking for anything similar to what he had seen in the Deathlands. His eyes traced the outlines of mangled pipes and rusted edges jutting out from the mounds of metal, imagining his father's body underneath one of the piles.

When the farm and wild game weren't quite keeping the family fed, Schultz had offered to pay Thomas a decent wage for organizing and taking inventory of the collection of rusted treasures. The piles were keeping visitors from knowing what was at the bottom, Schultz said, which meant that most mounds of scrap only grew larger.

They all knew that it wasn't really a necessary job, but Schultz was a friend – just as everyone in the town were friends – and he simply wanted to help Thomas out. Knowing that he would never accept a handout, Schultz just gave Thomas the first thing on the to-do list that he'd made for himself.

Thomas made progress much faster than Schultz expected. The speed and efficiency was mostly because Thomas wanted to prove his worth; that the payment to him was merited. Schultz had, on more than one occasion, mentioned that it was not a job that was under any sort of time constraints, and that he should save some of his energy for the never-ending work of a farm homestead. Thomas was much too proud, and refused to slow his efforts.

About a week into the side job, Thomas had realized that by pulling junk out of the bottom of the piles, he could avoid the time spent climbing to the top, bringing the materials down. He instead would cautiously remove items from the bottom, trying to create controlled avalanches of scrap. When all of the pieces scattered themselves on the ground, he could sort them quickly, tossing like-parts into a wheelbarrow to haul to their new respective areas. He had continued in this manner another week before the accident.

While tugging on a large object at the bottom of a pile, an avalanche erupted that he could not control. Letting go and jumping back to avoid collision, as was his usual reaction to unexpected results, he tripped. In the time that it took for his back to reach the dry grass, metal rained down on his body.

When he looked back, the part of the event that he shuddered most when retelling – but at the same time felt most compelled to tell – was the vivid sound of rusty metal scraping against rusty metal.

Jonah had overheard his father say that in those moments he had not prayed for safety, but that his demise would be quick, and his family taken care of. Soon after, however, the chaos ceased.

Pinned under the weight of the solid material, he called out for help, his voice straining from the pain. The junkyard was large – Schultz's home more than a hundred and fifty paces away. It was at least an hour before Schultz came upon the scene. He had not heard the weak screams, but had only noticed that it was unlike Thomas to take so long between hauling loads.

He pulled him out, removed some of the jagged metal embedded in the muscles in his legs and arms, and carried him to the center of town to the doctor. Doc Thorton did everything he could, but his right leg never recovered completely. His family constantly tried to help him see the bright side – they were all surprised that he had any use of it at all – but it was something that caused as much emotional pain as it did the physical pain of that day.

Jonah stared at the metal, imagining what it was like for his father. He shook his head, remembering why he was there today.

Surely I'll find some answers here, he reasoned with himself, refocused.

He hopped off his bicycle and bent down to pick up a few

pieces of wire fencing. He grabbed a nearby chain, considering if it would be a good replacement for the one on his bike – one that wouldn't squeak as badly. He held it up to the rusted gears on his two wheeled vehicle in comparison, and heard footsteps behind him.

"Jonah! I don't think it's a new chain you need – bring your bike over to my shop and we'll oil 'er up." Schultz smiled at him, wiping his hands on his shirt, leaving dirt on both the cloth and his skin.

Jonah stood up and tossed the chain back into the pile. "Yeah – I know I need to oil it, I just…" He paused, realizing that it was an offer for help, rather than a correction. "Thanks, Mr. Schultz."

"Stop with that 'Mister' stuff, kid – you're makin' me feel old," Schultz laughed. He extended his dirty hand and Jonah stood and shook it. "Good to see you, son. How's the family doin'?"

"They're good," Jonah replied, knowing the question was just a formality.

Since his father's accident, Schultz had always made sure that the Whitfields were taken care of. He would generally be over at the house before Jonah had even known that there would be reasons for concern.

They wheeled the bike toward the shop, catching up on the week that had occurred since they last saw each other. That is, catching up on everything but the Deathlands.

"…now, I don't figure you came 'cause of the bike chain, though – you've got plenty of grease in your shed. I checked on everything last time I was there," Schultz commented, then ended with a smirk. "But I did hear you comin' for a mile."

Jonah's mind raced, trying to figure out how to approach the subject of what he found in the Deathlands. He didn't know how to bring it up without explaining everything that he had seen, but wanted to keep as much of it a secret as he would be able. "Yes Sir... er..." Schultz raised his brow at the *Sir* remark. "I mean, yeah. I noticed the bike chain a couple of days ago on the way to hunt and I just haven't had time to fix it."

"Son, time's all any of us have *got!*" he snickered as he flipped the bike over onto a table in his wooden building as soon as they entered.

Jonah walked over to the bench and grabbed a small oil can and handed it to Schultz. "Right... I meant that I've had some other stuff on my mind since I got back from the hunt."

"Oooh," Schultz said knowingly, then chuckled. "The stuff on your mind wouldn't happen to have long hair and wear a pretty dress, would it?"

The young man smiled. "Not this time."

"Good," Schultz said as he greased the bike chain and gears. "That's out of my exper*tise*. Metal, rust – that's where everything makes sense to me. Women? For some reason they don't like bein' treated like junk. But that's all I'm used to workin' with! If you ever find one that does, you let me know. I ain't livin' alone cause I like it!" He chuckled again.

Jonah smiled. "Actually, Mr... Er, I mean Schultz. I wanted to ask you a question. Do you know what CHINA is?"

Schultz's eyes darted away from the gears. "China? Where'd you hear that?"

Jonah hesitated, not knowing if it was something only found in the Deathlands, wondering if he gave himself away. He nervously tried to respond, but nothing came out of his mouth.

"Did you see it on one of the pieces in my yard? Cause don't tell nobody, but I try to scratch that off if I see it."

"Oh?" Jonah finally stuttered. "Why do you try to scratch it off?"

Schultz made a slight frown, then changed the subject by wiping the oil from his hands and spinning the gears. "No squeak – she's good as new!"

"Thanks," Jonah said expectantly.

This time, it was Schultz's turn to hesitate. He flipped the bike back over onto the ground.

"Sir?"

Schultz sighed. "Well... You're not a kid any more. How old are you now?"

"Seventeen, sir."

"Old enough to stop callin' me *sir*, son!"

Jonah smiled, noting that he was still young enough to be referred to as *son*.

"I don't know how much you know about the history of this town. Or... this whole country, matter of fact."

"You mean, the ghost stories?" Jonah said as he tilted his head curiously.

"Lord Almighty, what do they teach kids in school these days?" Schultz wondered aloud, shaking his head with a sheepish look on his face. "But, I guess I can't dodge any of the blame either, scratchin' off words off all the metal in town."

"I'm confused, Schultz – and I don't know if you're actually trying to answer my question or if you're just avoiding it."

"Way to be direct, son," the older man said, nodding once. "It's a long story – one that I might can start, but your dad'll need to finish.

"The reason I scratch 'China' off the metal is 'cause it brings up questions about the past. And most people don't know a whole lot about the past. Honestly, for years folks tried to explain everything and pass it down.

"But after a while people started getting worried, 'cause we don't know everything – not that there's any way we could. People just get scared of things they don't know. Maybe that's why I don't have a wife... Most of the girls 'round here seem scared of all this metal. Think I'm just as rough as it."

Schultz seemed to daydream for a moment, but jerked his eyes back into focus.

"Anyhow, I can tell you some of what I know. Years and years ago, all this junk was just scattered all over the place. I mean everywhere. People hurt themselves on it. Some of 'em that got cut real bad would even die.

"My great-great-granddad started this here junkyard. When he was pretty young, he'd just gather up all the metal he could find. People were pretty happy for him to do it – they didn't see any use for it, so they thought he was just doin' it to clean the place up. They started givin' him wages to get it off their property, so for a while he was able to make a decent livin' doin' that instead of farmin', which is what his family had done for generations.

"What he didn't tell anybody is that he wanted to make stuff out of it. He'd clean it up real good, or melt it down, or what have you. He was able to make stuff that people could use, and got pretty good at repairin' stuff that people were already using. I guess you could say he was this town's first blacksmith. First one in a few days' journey, by all accounts. So – after all that time of people payin' him to get the junk off their land, later they started buyin' the same junk through the stuff he made, and payin' him for fixin' stuff."

Jonah noted that this skill had been passed down through ancestors, as Schultz was the man that everyone called when something needed repair. His shop was full of the town's broken plows, doors, and bed frames. Some would end up in the piles outside, destined to someday become something else completely. However, most items inside the building would take a day or two of tinkering and be sent back to the owner in exchange for a bushel of corn or a few large bottles of milk.

The town blacksmith, whom everyone called Brick, was the only other man who had similar skill – but even he would call on Schultz when a job had gotten the better of him. The nature of their work gave them a lot of time together.

Schultz continued speaking as he wiped the body of the bike.

"He spent most of his life gatherin' it up, and makin' stuff with it. When his boys got old enough, he tried to teach 'em how to do what he was doin'. They'd keep on gatherin' up metal and junk, and he'd show 'em how to make stuff out of it. Only his oldest son, Chester, really enjoyed it. As soon as the other boys got old enough, they got married and went back to farmin'. That was the only sure fire way of keepin' a family fed."

Schultz got up and moved to the opposite side of the shop, bent down, and started rummaging through items on a shelf under a workbench. "Chester, on the other hand, worked as hard as he could to get everything that people didn't want, figurin' that just about anything that people would throw away would be useful for *somethin'*.

"'Cause of that, he left his kids, and their kids – and eventually, me – a whole bunch of stuff. Some really useful, and some pretty worthless. And... a lot kinda in between." As Schultz searched through the objects, Jonah noticed a ring peeking out from under the bench, leaned against the wall. It looked similar to the wheel in the Deathlands, though much smaller. He didn't think it was the same as the one he'd seen here before, which gave him the feeling that it might not be so rare. Still, Jonah perked up at seeing this, waiting for the opportune time to ask a different question.

Schultz pulled out a large sphere on a metal frame. Setting it on the table in the middle of the room, where the bike rested minutes earlier, he spun the sphere.

"This here's a globe."

Jonah walked towards it curiously. "What's a globe?"

"It's a map." Schultz stopped the circling sphere, and pointed to an area of brown amidst a splash of dust covered blue. "That's China."

Jonah looked at the textured area, running his fingers over the surface, making trails in the dust. He noticed that on the base of the metal frame there were deep scratches. He could barely make out a few distorted letters. "I'm sorry, Schultz, but I still have no idea what you're trying to tell me."

Schultz let out a loud sigh. He then spun the globe around to the opposite side, and pointed at another mass of brown. "That's 'North America.' That's where we live. In *particular*, the United States of America."

Jonah furrowed his brow, narrowing his eyes trying to dig deep into his thoughts to pull out some sort of sense from what was being said. He didn't want to waste Schultz's time, but he definitely didn't want to leave without figuring out what any of the words meant when it was obvious that Schultz had some answers.

Noticing Jonah's long pause, Schultz continued.

"You've heard of oceans, right? Things that are like lakes with water you can't drink, but thousands of times bigger?"

"Yes... So, was China an ocean?"

"Well, I think the right question might be '*is* China an ocean,'" Schultz replied. "And the answer is no. All this blue color is water, and that brown stuff is land. Kinda hard to tell the difference with all the dust. This globe was made a long time ago. Years and years before Chester found it. Years before his dad started gatherin' junk. Back before the Resource War."

"Resource War?" Jonah asked blankly.

Schultz paused for a bit.

"Another long question for another time..." Schultz was trying to put boundaries on his explanations, but it was obvious that the single question required much more information than the simple answers that Jonah assumed would be found.

"When this map was made, we, America," he said, spinning

the globe for context, "we'd get a lot of our stuff from China."

"How?" Jonah didn't understand just how far apart the two lands were, but he knew that he absolutely couldn't travel there on his bike.

"More questions with long answers... At the time, we had these *huge* machines that could quickly travel long distances. By land, sea, and air."

"By air?" Jonah scoffed automatically in response. "Like riding a bird?"

"One thing at a time, son. If you get hung up on the details, you'll never get the whole picture." He continued, "all you need to know is that they'd make lots of the goods that the folks in America would use. They'd send it over here, but they'd put their name on it, to make sure that we *knew* who made it."

"Wait... I don't understand. Why would they make things for people in America, when they were separated by this ocean?" Jonah asked while pointing at the distance between the two countries. "Why wouldn't the people here just trade with their neighbors, and make the things themselves?"

"That's honestly a question that I'm not too sure of myself... I've been makin' things since I was a boy, so people have been comin' here for every odd and end you can think of. I figure if Brick and I weren't here, then somebody else'd pick up the slack and learn how to do it.

"But – as far as I can think is that I can't make things that look quite as... Well, even after all these years, some of it still looks polished. I guess they could of just been real good at makin' stuff, so folks started paying em to bring it over here to get the better, polished stuff.'"

Jonah wasn't necessarily satisfied with the answer. *Why wouldn't people in America just get better at making the same stuff? So that they wouldn't have to use the long distance traveling machines to bring them over?* Jonah didn't want to keep pressing, when it seemed like the answers to these questions weren't bringing him much clarity.

"You never told me where you saw the word 'China,' though, Jonah," Schultz said, remembering how they arrived on the subject.

Jonah cleared his throat, a habit he had when he lied since he was a child. "Uh, yeah, I just saw it on something in your yard." He didn't feel good about lying to Schultz, but he wasn't prepared to reveal what he had found without getting to explore it himself. "Under a bunch of other stuff – I could barely see it. I don't remember where, though..."

"Hmm... Okay. Tell me if you see it again."

"Absolutely, sir." Jonah put his hands on the handlebars of his bike, starting to wheel it silently out into the morning sun.

Schultz again chuckled at the word choice.

As he crossed the threshold to the outside, Jonah motioned toward the small metal ring leaned against the wall. "What would you use a ring like that for?"

Schultz walked to where Jonah was standing and noticed the ring. "I read about it in an old book – this is called a Valve. People would use them to close water pipes, or sometimes even doors."

"Doors? How would you open it?"

"You'd just turn it," Schultz said, picking it up and motioning it counter-clockwise. "I brought this one in here because I was going to try to use it on my shop door just for fun. It was too rusty, though, and it takes too much effort to open. Figured it wasn't worth it to break a sweat just to get inside!"

"Interesting..." Jonah crossed over the wooden boundary into the beaten path, feeling that he might have just found the answer to the reason for his visit. "Oh – how much for the wire fencing?"

"Nah, you don't need to pay me for that. Only, make sure you bring me another piece of your mom's famous pie when y'all get some apples in."

"Thanks! For the wire, oil and your help, Mr. Schultz!"

"Jonah – one of these days you're gonna stop calling me mister and sir!" He tried to stifle a grin, to act like it bothered him. "It's my pleasure, son. You know you're always welcome here."

.- .-- .- -.- .

Rolling the now silent wheels of the bike across his yard, Jonah pictured in his mind the valve protruding from the surface of the Deathlands. He had a vision of the wheel turning, opening a door into a cave – a cave that housed some terrible or wonderful beast. Perhaps an endless breeding ground of animals. Maybe the reason the game had not been near his usual hunting spot is because they'd all found a different way into some watering hole *below* the Deathlands?

Still, as much as he was ready to test out the theory of turning the valve, he had a handful of questions about what Schultz said. And about the story that Schultz had said his father would have to continue.

Across the yard, Jonah saw his father repairing a section of fence that held captive the family's small number of pigs. It was obvious that, because the pigs had rooted around one of the posts so long, it would only be another week or so before they would earn their freedom. Jonah ran over to grab the old fence post in place so that his father could drive the nails through the new wood. He was halfway sitting on a stool, his bad leg extended out of the way.

"Thanks bud," Thomas said, obviously happy to have an extra pair of hands. He sighed. "Takes me three times as long to do anything by myself anymore."

"But you still get it done, dad."

Thomas patted his son on the back instead of saying thanks.

The two worked silently. Jonah had long since learned not to ask his father if he needed help. He was a proud man, and didn't like the idea of not being capable enough for simple tasks on his own. If Jonah simply inserted himself into the work his father was doing, however, it was as if the movement of their hands were deep conversation.

"Get everything you need from Schultz's?" Thomas asked as they finished.

"Yeah – only enough for one more trap, but honestly I got

a little side-tracked."

"How so?"

"Well, he was telling me about where he got all the junk... And about China."

Jonah's father stiffened a bit and raised one of his eyebrows. "He telling you all his theories about the past?" There was a tinge of mockery in is voice.

"He was just telling me about a long time ago when people would get stuff made across the ocean and send it here instead of making it themselves." Jonah had no reason to doubt what Schultz had said – especially after seeing the globe.

"Oh, well yeah, I suppose *that* could be true."

"Why – what are his theories about the past?"

"I don't really want to get into all of it... There's a bunch of things that he says about it that seem a bit far-fetched. How'd you get on the subject?"

Jonah cleared his throat. "I... I saw 'China' written on something in his yard... Just wondered what it meant."

Thomas' posture eased a bit.

Jonah continued, "He said that you might want to finish telling me about it...?"

Thomas braced himself on his cane and started walking back to the house, their task complete. Jonah grabbed the remaining scraps from the old fence for firewood.

"Not right now... It's almost lunch time and your brother and sister will be home from the schoolhouse soon. No sense in confusing them."

CHAPTER THREE

Three days later, Jonah was legitimately in need of his satchel. After spending far too long butchering the deer, he realized just how reliant he was on his good knife. He had ruined one of his mother's kitchen knives trying to cut through the bone, for which he promised he'd find a replacement at Schultz's. He figured it was a good enough excuse to get back over there after he had another chance to open the object in the Deathlands.

He sat in the town's small chapel with his family, barely hearing Brother Philip's sermon. Harrison had a friend beside him, and the shushing sound to them from Jonah's mother was one of the few things that kept Jonah's mind in the room at all. The preacher's words drifted in and out between thoughts of the exposed object. He pictured it jutting out in the middle of the desolate plain, wondering how long it had been there.

His father hadn't brought up the past again, and Jonah had not expected anything different. He already had enough to chew on, mainly daydreaming about what would happen when he opened the 'valve,' so he didn't speak of it, either. But, still, he wondered about China, and oceans, and everything else Schultz had said. It might as well have been something that Brother Philip had talked about from the pulpit. He always spoke of places of the past – like Israel or Rome or Egypt – but this town was all Jonah had ever known. Anything more than a few days' travel could as easily have been just a story from one of the tattered books that took too much effort to read.

At least too much effort when there was already so much that needed to be done.

After his previous trip's kill was packed into the icebox and the smokehouse, he had worked feverishly to get ahead of his chores to create a bit of extra time for a trip. He wouldn't feel right about leaving something undone, knowing that extra work would fall on his father. His motivation helped him get done with double the work each day, so that – along with an icebox full of deer meat – there couldn't be any reason that he would need to stay. One of the things that his father *did* want to talk about was the frantic pace in which he worked; but something that Thomas Whitfield would never do is to tell someone not to work hard.

Before he realized Brother Phillip's sermon was over, his family stood up and were milling about, talking to their neighbors in the pews.

.- .-- .- -.- .

After Sunday dinner, he told his parents that he wanted to spend a couple of days simply resting. He loaded up his trailer with the new trap and a few day's worth of food and water and was pedaling toward the burning question in the ground. He left later in the day in order to camp and get an early start the next morning.

They were again confused, as he didn't normally talk about his hunting ground in a way that made it sound like a vacation. But they didn't question his motives – most likely because there weren't many other options as to why he would want to go there.

After camping by the edge of the Deathlands, he woke as soon as there was daylight breaking through his eyelids. Following the flags that were still protruding from the dense ground, he arrived at the object of his obsessive thoughts. It was unchanged.

He knelt beside the wheel and grabbed it with both hands, turning counter-clockwise instead of simply pulling up.

It still didn't budge.

He removed a thick metal rod from his trailer – another purchase from a previous trip to Schultz's that required nothing in return. Slipping the rod between the spoke of the wheel, he rested the end on the metal below. He braced himself against the rod with his legs strained and burning with the intent of rotating the wheel.

After tremendous effort the wheel moved with the subtle sound of two stones rubbing together for only a moment. Bits of rust dusted the shiny metal below. His body relaxed and his eyes continued to stare, perplexed. It had rotated, but not by much at all – about the length of a bullet.

He continued to push against the rod, his bent knees fighting to extend, digging his feet into the solid ground. It barely inched around, the rust slowly misting like saw dust.

Jonah moved to straddle the wheel, both hands around the body of his rod, bracing himself. He raised the thick metal above his head, keeping the spoke of the wheel in his sights, and brought it down as hard as he could. When it connected with the spoke, the wheel edged around slightly. Once again, raising his arms, he swung the makeshift hammer. The impact again inched the wheel around.

He repeated this process over and over, and eventually the wheel moved a bit more freely, the rust loosening up from the base.

He set the rod down beside him and brought up the edge of his shirt to wipe his brow, which was now covered thickly in sweat. He grabbed the wheel on both sides, and turned. The movement was slow and rough – as if he were grinding wheat between two stones – but it did move.

Eventually, it started spinning much more quickly, broken free from whatever friction that had held it back.

Then, all of a sudden, it stopped. He tugged again, but whatever had kept it in place before once again seemed to have it locked.

Frustrated, he stood straight up.

I can't start this over again, he mumbled to himself. *I don't have the strength to endlessly turn a useless piece of metal.*

But he knew that he would continue to turn it, even if it never gave him the answers to his questions.

He decided that he would simply tug on the wheel again – up, as he had done originally – wondering if it would open like a door in the way that Schultz had intended for the small one on the floor of his shop.

He planted his feet, grabbed the metal, and pulled. And the entire object lifted.

As it lifted, it swung on hinges still connected to the larger mass of metal below. He stepped back, lifting the heavy circle as far back as he could lead it, and it came to rest slightly past perpendicular to the ground.

Jonah stepped away, taking a few steps around to see clearly what it had uncovered.

He didn't know what to expect, but this was not it. Down the shaft of the seemingly unending hole, a ladder was affixed to the side. A strange soft glow dotted the walls, lighting the polished surface as far as his eyes could see down the abyss.

"Light?" he wondered aloud. "From the ground?"

He had only seen the darkness lit up by something other than sun or flame at Schultz's. In his home, he often showcased one of his experiments to intrigued visitors – something he called *Electricity*.

It took a great amount of effort to create the light from a glass bulb; he would extinguish the lamp and a volunteer would pedal a bike with no wheels, the chains and gears leading to a metallic box, with thin wires leading back to the bulb. It only took a moment for the bulb to come ablaze, lighting the whole room with absolutely no smoke.

If the volunteer continued, the bulb would even create heat – but as soon as the pedaling stopped, the fire inside the bulb would die away, leaving the room dark and silent until Schultz relit the lamp.

When Jonah was young, it simply seemed like a magic trick; a slight of hand, or a deception of the eye. In later years, Jonah would study the bulb much in the same way he stared at the Deathlands. But Schultz never revealed the secret; that is, assuming he even knew its secret.

In this glowing abyss, however, there was no effort. There was no repetitive noise of chain against gear – only a steady, low hum.

A strangely stale wind rushed out of the shaft in a constant breeze.

He hesitated at first, then reached out to touch the glowing air. He perched outside of the hole, running his fingers along the ladder and the smooth surface of the wall. Without thinking, he eased his foot onto the first rung of the ladder. Step by step, he descended into the strange endless compartment.

He stared around him, touching the soft glowing squares that projected light from the walls every few feet. They weren't warm to the touch, even though it seemed that they had been burning for some time. They didn't flicker as Schultz's bulb did, and the glow was much brighter.

In perfect, blocky letters set into the wall, he noticed the same peculiar message every fifth light: *Surface Duct 37C.*

He eventually made his way onto grated ground, with a tunnel continuing to his left and right. The low hum had now turned into a loud pulsing, seemingly coming from every direction. The lights littered the walls, illuminating pathways that split off in the corridor.

"What is this place?" Jonah whispered aloud as he took in his surroundings. This was completely unlike anything he had seen in his seventeen years. His world was filled with wood, earth, flame... The metal he interacted with, originating from the junk yard and possibly passing under the blacksmith's tools, was crude and dented.

Here, however, everything was pristine. Smooth. Polished.

He pulled out a strip of his shirt sleeve from his satchel, which he grabbed from the tree the night before, and tied it on the ladder. If the Deathlands, which he had gazed at for years, was disorienting, this labyrinth would have him wandering for the rest of his life.

Preparing another piece of fabric, he cautiously stepped down the hall, the shuffle of his soft soled shoes slightly echoing down the chamber. More letters lined the walls as he passed each option – *Ventilation Duct 37C (14), Maintenance Duct 37C (22), Resource Duct 37C (10).* Even though he recognized the language, none of it made sense.

On a whim, he took the orange material in his hand and pulled it through the grating at his feet. Tying it, he pointed the excess in the direction from which he came, the ladder still plainly in view. The opening in which he stood, *Ventilation*

Duct 37C (13), seemed as reasonable a choice to explore as any.

He stepped into the new tunnel slow at first, but picked up speed. If he was going to accomplish anything while there was still daylight outside, he could not waste too much time. He opted not to take any further deviations from this new path, to lessen the chance of losing his way.

After jogging a short distance, the path narrowed, and the ceiling sloped downward. The echo of his steps on the metal grating changed to the pounding of the solid floor he crossed over, and he lowered onto his hands and knees. There were no glowing lights ahead of him. Stopping for a moment, he noticed that the hum was behind him – but there was another strange sound coming from the passage before him.

Voices?

He couldn't quite tell yet... But he could swear that every so often, there was a mumbled sentence. He followed it.

"...so they just threw it in the trash shoot," a man's voice said, backed up by a belly laugh.

Jonah breathed heavily, sweat falling from his brow even though the temperature in his tunnel was cool and constant.

People? In the Deathlands? It's impossible.

"...looked at me, so I took control. Everyone was impressed with how I handled it," the man's voice continued.

"That's nice dear," said a woman, nonchalant.

As he continued on, he caught the scent of... food? But not quite the food he was used to – sweeter. He saw thin slits of light in the side of the tunnel and eased his eyes to look through.

The room was bright, with light emanating from the walls

which, strangely, looked as if they were windows overlooking a lush green valley. Colored squares lined the walls with rotating images of smiling uniformed people holding boxes or bottles. Words would spray across the walls, each seeming to compete with the other images for attention. Jonah couldn't help but stare at each of these surfaces, the voices from below his field of vision drowned out by the visual distractions.

Jonah shook his head, trying to tune out what he was seeing, and raised his head slightly to peer lower into the center of the room.

A family of four. Sitting at a table.

Their skin was pale, and their shiny silver clothing was formed perfectly to their large bodies. The man's black hair was slicked back and greasy, and he chewed with his mouth open. The woman's lips were bright and the shadows around her eyes were blue. The boy's back was to Jonah, and it looked as though he had some sort of large helmet that covered his eyes.

The man was touching a piece of black glass that was wrapped around his forearm. Each time he touched it, the glass seemed to respond – colors, animations swirling around his arm. Jonah noticed that all of them had this black object attached to them, and realized that the mother was staring at hers as well, occasionally swiping it as if to remove a fly with a finger.

Sweat beaded on the father's forehead in the cool temperature of the room. Glancing up for a moment, he gruffly commanded the boy, "What have we told you? No eyetiles at the table! We're having dinner as a family."

The boy sighed loudly as he removed the headgear, and then immediately started touching the glass on his forearm.

Over the boy's shoulder, now unobstructed by the boy's headgear, sat a girl Jonah's age.

Beautiful.

Her long sandy blonde hair was tossed around her shoulders, framing her pale face and green eyes. While her family was plump, their skin folding over the collars at their necklines, the girl had a small frame similar to those in his town. She held the physique of someone who knew the kind of labor his own family endured daily, but her pale skin was soft and hands uncalloused. Jonah's eyes traced the edges of the clothing clinging to her body, his face hugging the slits of the surface between them, when she glanced up.

He immediately retreated, quickly dropping from the narrow openings.

He stayed down for a moment, assuming that the beautiful girl had seen him – but nothing happened.

Moments later, he heard loud sniffing from toward the end of the table.

"Dawkin, did you sanitize yourself this morning?" the mother asked.

"Ugh... Yes I did," the boy whined.

"My nose tells me that you might not be giving me the truth," she said, the loud sniffs continuing.

"Did too! Check the visual records from this morning from the hallway! You can't make me undergo another sanitization until my scheduled time before lights out." The boy openly defied his mother, with no remorse in his voice.

The father's voice arose, alongside a new set of sniffing.

"Are you sure, Dawkin? I smell something strange too..."

Jonah knew what the problem was. Him.

The air filling the chamber was stale and sweet – but his body and clothes smelled of sweat. On the surface, it was expected. Down here, Jonah assumed the odor of work might not be common, judging by the frames of the three family members.

The boy squeaked his chair back from the table as Jonah peeked through the slits once again, making sure the green eyes of the girl weren't pointed in his direction – even though part of him wanted them to be.

The entire family was watching the boy stomp his feet over to one of the colored panes on the wall, tap aggressively, and turn around with his arms crossed. Jonah noticed that his round face had a look of indignation, and his nose was turned up. Dawkin, about the same age as Jonah's brother, seemed to have no resemblance to the beautiful creature that had been sitting across from him at the table.

The glass behind the boy duplicated the boy, showing him emerging from a room with wet hair, a cloth draped around his body. It was as if his identical twin was being watched through a window.

"See?! I told you!" he yelled at his parents. "You are so stupid!"

Jonah was taken aback by the volume and the boy's disrespect. He expected the parents to react the way any parent in his town would have reacted – with a swift smack to the behind. Or, to match the intensity of the defiance, a deserved slap in the face.

Instead, the father simply stated, "You're right - sorry. It must be the ventilation system acting up... I could bring it to the attention of the rest of the Regulation Committee, but if it's within reasonable levels we might get a complaint ticket... I'm sure someone will take care of it, so it might be best to wait it out a bit."

"That's for the best, Quilen," his wife said as her eyes returned to the arm glass.

The boy returned to his seat, beaming because of his parents' defeat.

Jonah's mouth was open in amazement of the exchange that he had just witnessed, taking in just how different the world was that he had stepped into.

The father puffed on a strange tube that glowed blue, releasing smoke through his nose.

The substance on their plates was anomalous to the Whitfields' meals. There were three different colored pastes sectioned off on the round platters in front of them in equal portions, each resembling the consistency of mashed potatoes that had been squeezed through a tube. He had the feeling that someone had ground each of the portions that were served, so that they would not have to be bothered with chewing their food.

Jonah watched the family as if they were a performance, like the traveling troubadours that would pass through his community, who would only ask for a meal and lodging for the night in return.

Except in those cases, the performers knew of the

audience's existence, and would direct their attention to what they wanted seen. In this case, the actors were simply being, which was far more foreign than any of the plays he had ever seen.

The girl, completely out of place and with her plate still half full, sighed and softly requested, "May I be excused?"

Her voice, unlike her brother's, was polite and fragile. The words seemed to flow like silk through the slits in the wall in which Jonah was watching, gracing his ears like a gentle breeze. They held the sound of dissatisfaction, which was the only emotion in the room that he had yet connected with.

"And miss dessert?" the father scoffed, his belly bouncing only once.

"I'm... I'm not very hungry," she answered, as if it wasn't so much that she wasn't hungry, but wasn't content with pre-chewed paste.   Or the subject matter of the meal's conversation.

"One of these days you'll learn to appreciate the finer things in life – like dessert. There were times in history when people had to work assignment shifts all day for a reward like this," he said as if reading a prepared speech. "Of course, if you want to visit a few housing sections away, you can find the laborers that still have to," he chuckled.

As he spoke, he pushed the surface of the table with the tip of his finger, and a small opening appeared in front of him. A tube curved out of the hole, ending just above an empty section of his plate. After pushing once again on the table, a red gooey substance slipped out of the pipe, piling on top of the end of his fork. Dessert.

"You'll wake up and realize that everything you could have ever wanted has been here the whole time!"

The girl patiently waited until he had shoved a glob of the slime into his mouth, then repeated, "So, may I be excused?"

"Yes, Talitha, you may be excused," her mother answered, barely looking up from her arm glass.

Talitha. The name echoed through Jonah's head like musical notes. *That fits her perfectly.*

She stood, grabbing her plate and a cup of blue liquid, and walked toward one of the windows that spanned from the floor to the ceiling. She pressed against the glass, and a large pane went black, the valley disappearing, and folded out toward her.

She tossed the contents of her hands – plate, silverware, cup, uneaten paste – down into the opened compartment, which closed slowly. As soon as it connected to the rest of the black wall, the scenery reappeared.

Talitha turned and walked out of the room, much to Jonah's dismay. He found that – even though he had just discovered a family that lived below the surface of the Deathlands, which should keep his interest for years – he was immediately bored with the three family members that remained in the room. All of them simply stared at different glass surfaces, not speaking, mesmerized.

Jonah slowly slid along the surface of his chamber, hoping that the slits he'd been staring through weren't the only ones. He silently moved through the darkness, his years of patiently hunting aiding him in his motions. He found deviations in the path, but he thought it wise to stay straight – he could explore the other options when he was better prepared, and knew the pathway back.

It didn't take long for him to be peering through another set of slits – a hallway of some kind – but it didn't hold his attention. He continued to move.

Nearing another set of slits, he heard the girl humming a slow melody, the notes hanging in the air like clouds. He eased his face to the holes in the wall that separated, and watched her move about the room. He gathered that it was where she slept – alone – which was another surprise to him, as everyone he knew shared their rooms with their siblings, if not their parents, too.

Talitha laid down in the floor, and touched her arm glass gracefully. With each motion, something in the room changed. First, the doorway she walked through sealed shut on its own. Second, the bright lights that were coming from various parts of the room faded to nothing. Third, the entire room was covered in the night sky.

.- .-- .- -.- .

Jonah didn't know how long he had been staring at the girl lying in the middle of the floor, her chest rising and falling slowly from her breath, but he jolted suddenly when the seal over the entryway of the room broke, and bright light poured in. Her mother walked in.

"Looking at the stars again, dear?"

Talitha, who had obviously fallen asleep, rubbed her

emerald eyes, waiting for them to adjust to this forced dawn. She paused for a moment before responding. "I wish I could really look at them."

"But sweetheart, you *are* looking at them. That's exactly what they looked like before the Surface's End."

"You know what I mean, mom. I wish I could go to the surface, lay on the actual ground. Breath fresh air, look at the *actual* stars—"

"You really should listen to your father," her mother interrupted, sitting on the edge of the bed. "He's right, you know. You should enjoy the life that we have here, and understand that you have everything at your fingertips. Talking about the surface isn't going to change it. *Fresh* air... You wouldn't be able to choke out a single breath." Jonah's face twitched in surprise. "You've seen the video feeds – it's not safe. Nothing but fire and radiation. You can see the good parts of the past on the digitiles, and you don't have to think about the bad parts of it. It's *better* than reality."

"But what's the point?" Talitha sighed. "What's the purpose in reliving the same day every day. Is studying in classes about history supposed to frighten me into contentment? Training for a position in the Regulation Committee so that I can spend my life in a decision chamber, acting like my time matters. Everybody's busy, but nobody actually does anything – the Facility takes care of everything. Nothing anybody does actually makes a difference." She looked down, slumping her shoulders.

"Talitha, I don't want to hear that talk from you anymore," her mother reprimanded, her voice short. Her face held a look of indignation. "There are plenty of people who wish that they were the same status class as we are – that their children could automatically be appointed to the Regulation Committee. If your great-great-grandfather hadn't headed up the Complaint Committee, then you very well could've ended up as a laborer. And you definitely wouldn't get to complain about *dessert*."

The girl sighed. "I'm not trying to complain about what I have, mom. I just... I..." She obviously didn't know what to say that would make it seem like she was happy. "Thanks, mom. Both you and dad do a lot to make sure that Dawkin and I are comfortable."

Her mother looked pleased. "That's more like it," she said, a smile curling up at the edges of her lips. "If I recall, you have a Historical Tax exam to study for before bed, right?"

Talitha stood up, stretching.

"Yes. I'll bring up the lectures on the digitiles."

Her mother kissed her forehead and walked out of the room. Talitha touched the glass on her arm and the entry way sealed again but she then dissipated the stars and brought the lights up in the room. Jonah squinted at the immediate change, his eyes having been adjusted to the twilight that had been emanating from the room.

"Useless," Talitha mumbled. "Why do we have to learn about how the Leaders saved us from the Surface's End through taxation, when there's nothing to tax now?"

Within moments, a life-size man appeared on the far wall, books surrounding him, and a voice announced "Twenty Second Century Taxation, lecture six." The man on the wall, with a different voice, began droning about earning laws, and how, in some distant past, the rich were destroying the poor. Jonah started edging away when the voice lectured on how the Leaders leveled the playing field, and that taxes and redistribution were the only way that civilization could be sustained.

He pictured his home covered in endless flames, wondering what the other word her mother used – *Radiation?* – meant.

After only a few feet, he pulled out a piece of cloth still in his satchel and tied it on a small metal loop in the wall of the tunnel. He would definitely want to return to this place. He started his movement once more.

The thought occurred to him that he'd be content to simply watch the porcelain skinned girl for the rest of his time in the tunnels – and possibly his life – but realized that he needed to find out more about his new surroundings while he still had daylight above.

Assuming he still did have daylight above. He tried to estimate the time, knowing that if he were to emerge from the tunnel with only the moonlight overhead, he could wander in the Deathlands aimlessly. And camping in the Deathlands was only slightly less disenchanting.

It had at least been a few hours since he had descended down the glowing shaft, because his stomach was quietly declaring that his small breakfast was long ago.

Jonah glanced into the room in which the family had dined earlier. Where it once was bright, the dark glass covering the walls only faintly reflected dancing lights from deeper down the connected hall. When first looking upon the room, he was quite amazed that, underground, they were able to see a lush valley through the glass walls.

However, after seeing so many dancing images in both this room and in the bedroom of the girl he realized it was some sort of magic that all of the walls possessed. Much more miraculous than the cold, constant burning lights in the tunnel in which he descended to this world.

He crawled towards his origination in the 'duct,' as it had been labeled. The tunnel opened up, and he was once again standing on a grated floor. He passed the end of the tunnel, where he found the orange cloth from his shirt tied to the ground, and looked to his left to see the ladder. He instead turned to the right, grabbing an apple from his satchel.

He replayed the family's earlier conversation in his head, recognizing that they had talked of others. Others that must also reside in the series of tunnels. It seemed incredibly unlikely that anyone could survive in an enclosed area such as this at all, but even more impossible that they could survive alone.

The surprise that there were *more* people underground was less than the initial shock of stumbling upon the family. But still, he felt it was strange to be walking around, who knows how far underground, searching for people.

Between bites of his apple, he tried to stay focused on his surroundings, realizing that wandering aimlessly could result in a much longer stay than he anticipated.

When he took the last bite of his apple, he threw the core in his satchel and paused in front of an opening marked *Resource Duct 35C (15)*.

He removed two more pieces of orange cloth from his bag,

tying one to the grating in the main tunnel towards the ladder, and one just inside the duct, which looked to him as simply a new tunnel opening. Everything looked the same, so he knew that he had to mark every move he made – it would be unwise to assume he'd remember the correct numbers and letters associated with the different duct entrances.

Walking only a short distance, he noticed a faint smell in the air. In relation to the rest of the stale oxygen of the tunnels, or the sweet aroma near the family, it was familiar. But it was not to say it was entirely familiar – merely that the quality seemed more appropriate for the land near his home than in the metal cage he was currently in.

The further he walked, the stronger the smell. He couldn't quite place it, for among the recognizable odor was a concoction of something... else.

At a dead-end, he reached a window unlike the polished, pristine glass that he'd seen in the family's rooms – one with the dirt and fog that he was accustomed to. The liquid stains on it made it hard to see through, but he did see movement.

Jonah noticed that the window was set into a door, and that the handle to the door was barely soiled. Cleaner than almost anything he'd known on the surface, it still seemed dirty in this sterile environment – though it fit with the window.

He resolved to try to open the door as quietly as possible, hoping that he could still count on his hunter's instincts and patience to not be noticed. He placed his fingers on the handle, and slowly pulled it down, making sure that any squeak that it made would not compete in volume to a scampering field mouse.

Inch by inch, he reached the end of the handle's rotation, and barely cracked the door open.

And immediately vomited.

CHAPTER FOUR

Jonah had been around livestock all his life. When he was a child, barely old enough to walk, his mother would let him pet the pigs and chickens on the family farm while his father fed and watered them. Later, when the family would visit neighbors, Jonah would inevitably wander off to converse with the area animals – bleating with goats, mooing at calves – often resulting in a quick swipe on the behind by his mother and lectures on not wandering off.

As he grew, he involved himself in everything his father did. While the majority of that time was in the vegetable field, the beginning and end of the day was always spent making sure the animals had provisions or thanking the hens while gathering their eggs. When he was the age of eight, he was given the task of killing his first rooster.

This task was uncomfortable for him, even though he'd seen his father and mother do it countless times before. He felt it to be a great honor, however, because it was an acknowledgement that he was nearing adulthood – that his contribution to the family was more than simply tiny jobs that merely wouldn't be completed otherwise.

Prior to catching the chicken, Thomas had pulled Jonah aside to thank the Lord, "who made the chickens for them to eat." He explained to him that the reason they fed the animals well, and treated them better than an irresponsible farmer at the other end of the town, was that it was a life – and that life was precious, no matter what form it came in. Jonah was quick to note each time he passed by the farm of the man his father referred to - the animals had escaped or were violent or were dying of disease. The Whitfield's animals were always plump and happy.

His brother and sister were still much too young to handle a knife, so as Jonah, guided by his father's hands, finished the grown up work, he beamed at his siblings, hiding the edge of sadness deep in his stomach. They whined to their mother that they, too, were old enough to help. They were obviously not content in their mother's answer that Jonah was older, and that they'd get to help one day, as well.

Their father laughed loudly, letting all of them know that it wouldn't be very long before Jonah didn't think of it as special, but rather just another chore on the list.

By the time Lillian had reached age eight, she no longer found the same allure in the task, and begged her parents to "skip over her."

In the years following, Jonah had butchered everything from rabbits to bulls, and as his father predicted, it was done only out of necessity and not out of excitement. He had seen the bloodiest of slaughters, but nothing prepared him for what he stared at through the now wide-open door of *Resource Duct 35C (15)*.

The huge room before him was stuffed from wall to wall with different animals, each with a cage that was barely larger than the beasts themselves. The cages were stacked on top of each other like bricks, with the larger animals at the base.

The stench that had been faint in the tunnels was overwhelming, and Jonah covered his mouth and nose with the fabric from his shirt. He had been in unkempt pig pens and shoveled horse manure, but the smell of those experiences could not prepare him for the pollution that was burning the walls of his nostrils.

The animals barely moved, and as Jonah approached the nearest cow, he could see that each of the bodies were restrained. Tubes were buried deep in the heifer's mouth, pumping in water and food. Another tube was in the animal's anus, sucking out excrement.

Needles were embedded in various points of flesh, some connected to bags of clear liquid that dripped in a steady rhythm, and others that flowed with a steady stream of blood into unknown cracks below the floor. The tubes were not foolproof, and anything that did not reach it's intended destination fell on the cages below. This particular cow was caked with the dung of a pig above, and from possibly several animals above that.

The eyes of the beasts around him stared blankly, no doubt looking at the same thing that they'd seen for their entire lives – except for some that now saw a visitor that gazed back in helpless disgust.

While he was scanning the room, several large contraptions that looked like piles of metal in Schultz's junkyard – except that the light reflected off their polished surfaces – slid against the ceiling suddenly as if they had minds of their own. Jonah ducked out of sight, afraid that the mess of tubes and slick metal would see his movements; he did not know if they were somehow alive. Still, he edged curiously toward them, staying close to the animal cages, to see if he could observe their movements.

The contraptions extended from the ceiling. They shined a harsh red light momentarily on the top bar of the cages at the far end of the room, and after a beep, latched onto the corners of those cages. One by one, and with uncommon speed, each cage was lifted and placed onto a narrow black section of the floor that was moving as if it were a stream. The cages, caught up in the current of the black floor, reached the wall, which opened up like a curtain over a window and enveloped them.

After the entire first row of animals was gone, the contraptions detracted. Sliding against the ceiling into the corner, they became lifeless, as if they were never more than piles of shining junk. Jonah stared at them expectantly, wondering if they would spring to life the moment he moved.

A shrill sound echoed through the room, causing him to once again shrink against the cages.

Beep... Beep... Beep....

His eyes widened, afraid that the noise was an indication of his existence. He shot his sight to the entrance, the door that had revealed the atrocious room. He could sprint and possibly get back to the ladder before he was caught.

As he took his first step, red light pulsated from the wall where the animals disappeared. Contents of the entire room – all of the cages containing animals – moved forward. The metal of the cages screeched, the sound reverberating against the wall near Jonah's ears.

The far row that had disappeared had been replaced by the second row. The row on the opposite side of the room was empty for only a moment, as another row of cages, also stacked to the ceiling, slid into place from an opening in the side wall.

When he touched the door handle, the beeping and light ceased. Jonah opened the door and shot one foot into the tunnel, but he hesitated when he realized that, besides the slight shudders of the animals and the sound that echoed from the cages, the room was still.

He scanned the room again, looking for signs of his discovery – of signs that someone (or something) was searching to grab him like one of the cages.

Nothing.

It seemed his presence in the room was still nothing more than a hidden observer. As if the movements were automatic, and that they had been repeated countless times before his arrival and would do so after he left.

He looked at the newly positioned row of animals at the edge of the room. Some were slightly smaller than those in the first row – the ones that disappeared through the wall. The thought occurred to him that this was a holding cell, a place to maintain them after the animals had matured. That by the time the new row reached the black stream on the floor, those smaller animals would also be the age for slaughter.

He stepped back into the room, letting the door again close behind him with less care than before. Either his presence was unknown or simply ignored – but either way he felt a bit more freedom to examine the process of what had happened.

He swiftly walked to the area where the animals had melted into the wall. The black floor had stopped moving, and he attempted to dip the tip of his shoe into it. It was solid. He put his hands on the wall, though the surface looked more like cloth than the surrounding metal. He pushed it away, as if pushing aside the quilt on his bed, and peeked through.

The cages had been taken off the black floor, presumably by several contraptions that were piled up in the corners of the ceiling, and sat scattered along its path. The cages had several new tubes protruding from them, with red liquid flowing from the cages to holes in the floor. All of the smaller animals – rabbits, chickens, cats – were slumped in their cages, lifeless. The larger animals – cows, pigs, sheep, dogs – were swaying woozily while their blood was taken from them. One by one, animals gave up the fight and fell to the floor of their cages.

Jonah walked alongside the black path – not stepping on it for fear of it springing to life once more – helplessly watching each of the animals die.

The smallest cages were each being opened with metal arms from nearby poles, and the animal inside was quickly tossed to and fro. The tubes and needles that were connected to its body were ripped away. The carcass was dipped into a bubbling clear liquid that made Jonah's skin burn from a few feet away.

After being extracted from the liquid which had removed feathers and fur, another metal arm with a spinning blade cut the corpse in half. Some of the bones were ripped out by dozens of arms with attached knives and tools, taking only a few seconds. The largest bones fell into a hole in the ground, while many bones remained in the meat.

Jonah looked at all of the animals undergoing the slaughter, realizing that each station of metal arms was slightly different – some merely in size, but some in arrangement – to be specific to each animal.

All of the meat from each animal was thrown into large funnels, including skin and organs that were missed by the previous machines. Many different animals were tossed into the same containers. The containers erupted with the grinding and scratching sounds of metal against metal and bone. He could clearly see that as each piece of flesh was ground up, it would press through another clear tube. Staying away from the sharp metal objects, he followed the path of the clear tubes of meat.

After a series of automatic mechanical bowls that mixed in powders and liquids, the contents of the tubes terminated in at least thirty different heated vats. In those vats, more liquids and powders were added, this time changing the pink flesh into various colors, and emitted different smells.

In bold white letters against the gray surface on the outside of each vat, an announcement was made as to the new contents.

Food Substance

Each was marked with a number and letter, much like the tunnel markings. Once filled, a vat and its heating element would move along toward the wall, with other containers previously mixed.

Walking to the end of the line of vats, he realized that they were filled with the same pre-chewed paste that he had seen Talitha's family eating.

Jonah vomited once more.

.- .-- .- -.- .

Jonah sucked as much fresh morning air into his lungs as possible as he sat by the fire near his hunting tree. After resurfacing the night before, he had tried to eat the food that he brought with him in his satchel, but on it lingered the smells of the slaughter room. Instead, he had grabbed his gun and was able to shoot a squirrel for his dinner, and picked some nearby greens.

He had thanked God as his father had taught him – this time with a very new appreciation for where his food came from. The thought of grinding it into the paste had made his already sick stomach ache once more.

Cleaning the squirrel and roasting it over the fire, he had eaten almost the entire animal, filling his completely evacuated stomach. Even with the meal and finishing off his canteen, he still had the taste of acid in his mouth, and the smell of the powders and liquids in his nose.

After sleeping under the stars that he was so used to, he had considered simply going back to town to tell his family what he had seen. There were so many things to tell them, and he wasn't sure if he could handle it on his own anymore.

But this morning, the only thing that drew him back underground was the thought of seeing Talitha once again. He wondered if the reason she didn't seem to enjoy the family dinner was because she knew about the series of tubes it traveled through to arrive at the table, and because she knew of the cages where the paste originated from. He hoped that was at least one of the reasons why.

Picking from the bones of the squirrel, he stamped out the fire and jumped back on his bike toward the ladder in the middle of the Deathlands.

After descending once again, he immediately found his way to the slits in the wall of Talitha's dining room.

Talitha's father, Quilen, was sitting in his place at the table, hunched over. His shirt was covered in sweat, and his skin was paler than the previous day with a tint of green. Each breath that he took seemed to take all of his effort, and his body shivered.

"...everybody was sick," he whispered to his wife, as if that effort alone was too much. "The department head of the entire Sector Planning Committee was throwing up. So, Clarito sent everyone back to their housing units."

His wife looked tired and a bit disheveled, but nowhere near the condition of her husband. Her voice didn't seem to require as much strength to form words. "Do they know what happened? Why everyone is... so bad? I've never seen it like this." She looked worried, but Jonah couldn't tell if it was because of what was on her mind or what was in her body.

"I... I..."

Quilen sneezed, streaking mucus across the glass table.

"I don't know exactly, but the computer said that there was an *'introduction of a consumable foreign contaminate'* in the food substance last night... I don't know why the forefathers didn't program the computers to speak in plain English," he answered as he, much slower than the dinner before, pushed buttons on the table that caused a metal arm to appear from the ceiling with a cloth in its grip.

As it cleaned the table, he continued. "Nobody knew what it meant – even the top Technology Maintenance Officer from Sector 14D... He's supposedly the one who knows the most about The Facility for at least two hours' ride on the Magnet Tram. They actually physically brought him in - not just on video link.

"The big shot said that there had to be an error in the computer, because the food substance processing is foolproof. Said that it must have been one of the gathered resources that has something wrong with it, and didn't get thrown out before preparing this morning's breakfast."

"Oh..." His wife was obviously concerned.

"Don't worry, Gabet," he comforted her between shivers. "They'll figure out which resource it was and ban it. They already permitted the computer to release a vapor cure in the ventilation ducts before the Officer got there. It'll show up in the food by tonight and the next batch of Chemvapor – for the entire facility, just in case."

"It just seems so strange," she said staring into the glass walls, which seemed as if they were overlooking a serene lake. "I can remember one or two people sick my whole life. One at a time – never a group of people. And... never this—"

"Never this bad, I know. We'll be fine," Quilen coughed, not seeming to believe his own words. "Right before I had to leave, they were in the process of forming a subcommittee from the Wellness and Pain Management Committee to research it. Must have been a non-synthetic that somehow hasn't been replaced yet. They'll take care of it. I suppose that one bout of fever in all of my fifty-two years is manageable, right?"

Jonah realized that there was sarcasm in his voice, as if one fever in fifty-two years was *not* manageable.

Jonah thought it very strange as well. Not in the way that Gabet found it to be strange, but in that they were so surprised by a virus that had spread among a group of them. Jonah had recalled countless times when he was required to stay home from the schoolhouse because of other children being sick, and from catching a fever almost every time one of his siblings had one.

He had always assumed that was simply a part of life – that some days were meant to be less than ideal, so that the *normal* days were quite positive in comparison. He never felt more energetic than he did a few hours after a fever broke, and would try to remind himself of that release for days after. As if the gift of that reminder was buried in temporary illness.

He knew, though he tried to shove it into the recesses of his mind, that he was the cause for the outbreak.

If the average fifty year old had not been sick for his entire life, then he could easily assume his presence amongst the animals introduced what they considered a *foreign contaminate.* Especially his vomit.

He continued down the duct, passing the dim hallway, and made his way to the slits of Talitha's room. She wasn't there.

Disappointment washed over him – he was hoping to see her lying on the floor, staring at the simulated stars once again. But he knew that she must have chores of her own, and he couldn't expect her to be in the room every time his eyes peered through the slits. But, still, he had hoped.

He continued down the duct, further than his first venture, and peered through slits into dark, glassy, empty rooms. It appeared as though the walls only danced with images and colors while people were present, perhaps awakened by the glass surfaces on their forearms as in Talitha's room.

After his eyes adjusted to the darkness, he saw another bedroom – likely for Talitha's parents considering the enormous size of the bed – and room after room of objects for which he did not know the purpose.

One had a small section of floor that reminded Jonah of the moving black stream in the livestock room, but it was only wide enough for one person, and only long enough to take three or four short steps. It was one of the few objects he could see that had a thin layer of dust on it.

Another room had a work bench, but had no tools on it, only panels of glass about the size of the books he had read - or at least was supposed to read - in the schoolhouse.

There were no slits in the walls for a distance, and then

Jonah came across another dining room setting. In this was another plump man, wearing the exact same jumpsuit as Talitha's family. His head was hovering over a section of the wall that was protruding. It looked like the same box that Talitha had thrown the contents of her meal the previous day. This man was also sweating, pale, and green. He, too, was sick.

Jonah felt sympathy for them, and regret that he was the cause for their illness. Though, in truth, he was confused that they weren't sick all of the time from the 'food' they consumed.

He turned around, and made his way all the way back to the tunnel with the surface ladder and numerous choices of ducts. After casually looking at his options, he settled on adventuring through an opening labeled *Waste Duct 36C (9)*.

After marking it with more cloth, and realizing that the material he had repurposed from his shirt sleeves were nearly gone, he walked down its path.

He came upon another dead-end door, this time with no grimy window. He filled his lungs and held his breath, assuming that whatever he discovered behind the door would be another cause for disgust.

Slowly pulling the handle down and easing the door open, he took the room in, which was again devoid of people. It was apparently a junkyard, but much different from the mass of twisted rust at the edge of his own hometown. He was hopeful that he'd be able to find some sort of treasure to take back to Schultz's to trade for more information – without surrendering the location from where it came.

The first thing he noticed was that more refuse was pouring into the room through various chutes in the wall. Similar items were somehow sorted and diverted to different piles on the floor.

The second, more frightening thing he saw was that objects hovered in mid-air.

Silverware, plates, and various pieces of metal floated from the ground up to the ceiling. As he stepped into the room, he was distracted by not only the floating objects, but also that the walls had a different kind of shine to them. They seemed more like skin than anything else.

Before he noticed, his satchel had floated above his head, and the strap wrapped around his arm and neck. It continued to rise, and the strap continued to tighten around him. He grabbed the straps with both hands and pulled, trying to keep the unseen force from not only claiming the bag, but strangling him in the process.

In a jerk, the flap of the satchel opened up, and while a few items spilled down – what little food that he hadn't eaten from the previous night, the remaining sleeve cloth, a horn filled with gunpowder – other items spilled *up*. Each individual bullet that he had stashed in his pack quickly rose and stuck to the ceiling, scraping along the surface as if herded by an unseen shepherd. As soon as his knife flew toward the top of the room, the satchel fell lifeless at his side.

Quickly grabbing the objects that fell down, he climbed the piles of soft garbage to intercept the knife from wherever the herd's destination was. He could live without the bullets, though they would most likely cost him more to replace than he was comfortable with, but he had already seen how important his knife had been to him by its absence.

He followed the knife, stepping through mushy refuse mounded up high enough for the ceiling to be only just out of his reach. He pushed floating metal objects out of the way, at times grabbing them expecting to climb them like ladder steps, but none of them held his weight. He recognized that there were no other sharp objects, besides his knife, following the path of the bullet shepherd. Even the forks had dull tips that would barely spear a piece of tender meat.

When he found himself at the corner of the room, he jumped at the knife, not wanting to lose it through the hole in the wall that all of the pieces of metal were falling through.

He was not successful.

Instead, he fell into a pile of pre-chewed paste, bone, and discarded clothing. Watching the knife disappear through the hole, he quickly recovered to his feet. He felt along the flesh-like wall to see if he'd be able continue to follow his possessions, still looking up. He found another handle and swung the entrance to the next room open, disregarding the care that he had taken for all of the previous doors.

When he entered the room, all of the herded metal from the ceiling was laying on yet another river-like conveyor belt that was moving toward the center of the room. He grabbed his knife and ran to scoop up several bullets, but stopped quickly before the objects on the belt passed under a clear liquid – the same liquid that he felt burn his skin in the slaughter room. It was obvious that all of the objects were passing under to be cleaned, though Jonah was sure that if he passed his hand underneath the flowing solution, the flesh on his bones would disintegrate. Even standing a few feet away, his skin sizzled.

Jonah realized that he was getting sloppy with his actions in his haste. He was relieved that, even with the commotion that he had caused in the garbage room and his rush through the door in the fleshy wall, no human eyes had fallen upon him. Though, as in the slaughter room, he couldn't help but feel that at every moment, pieces of machinery had their eyes on him.

His gaze darted around his new surroundings. Throughout the room, items were being sprayed down with liquids. Mechanical arms were sorting similar materials, sometimes ripping objects apart or grinding them up, or simply pushing them aside to be handled further down the process.

He moved toward a pile made up of clothing that looked like the silver garb that Talitha's family wore. He assumed that all of the underground inhabitants dressed alike.

Jonah sifted through the pile, holding certain pieces close to his body. It took him a quite a while to find an outfit that wasn't too large, and when he slipped into one it still sagged all around him, though it was obviously for someone shorter than he. He wadded up his clothes in the corner. There were no pockets or pouches in the silver fabric, so he reluctantly sat his satchel on top of his own small pile of clothing. He stuffed the pile between two boxy machines, pushing his belongings out of sight.

The cleaning liquid that remained on his new uniform seemed to seep from the fabric into his skin, as if they had been soaked in boiling water, but were at the same time cooler than his body. The stinging sensation lasted only momentarily. He didn't know what his plans were, but he did know that he'd prefer to blend in if he were seen - and he thought perhaps the liquid would mask some of his odor, so the short burning pain was worth it.

After peering through a window, he slowly opened the door to a bright, metallic hallway. He heard footsteps echoing down the corridor, far enough away that he knew that he'd have plenty of time to make his escape if he were seen. Or – he assumed he'd have plenty of time.

What are you doing? he contended with himself, his thoughts screaming. *You should just watch them through windows and cracks.*

He didn't know what compelled him to place himself in possible danger – he had no idea what would happen if he were caught. For all he knew, he wasn't the first visitor from the surface, so they might be expecting him. And it wouldn't be long before they found him out to be the reason for the illness.

What if they chain you up? Or worse – throw you into one of those animal cages?!

Despite the obvious problems that could arise, he knew that he wouldn't be satisfied simply observing as if the people that lived here were clouds in the distance, trying to guess what shapes they were taking.

He stepped completely through the door, noting the letters near the handle. *Sanitation Center 36.* He hadn't picked up the remaining sleeve cloth in the Waste Duct, so he couldn't go far – otherwise the strange letters and numbers would start to melt together and he would have no idea how to get back.

Glancing down the hall, he could see large men in the

distance, walking busily to and fro.   Each was staring and touching at the glass on their arms.   He didn't want to chance it at the moment, but he felt that it would be a possibility to simply walk right by them, and they wouldn't be distracted from the glass.

He heard a steady pulsating noise – close to the honk of a goose, but so consistent that he didn't think it was made by a living thing – and walked towards it.   He soon ended up in a room with black glass all over the walls.   One wall was covered with glowing circles.   One circle projected a deep red glow each time the noise pulsed.   The noise wasn't coming directly from the button, but it was obvious that they were in some way tied to each other.

The black glass scrolled letters across the walls in various colors.

Resource Collection: 57%

Ventilation: 84%

Sanitation Systems: 75%

The letters of *Water Reservoir: 7%* were also blinking in red to the tempo of the noise.

The walls seemed to constantly post various statuses, but they didn't make any sense to Jonah.   The only thing in the large, glowing room that Jonah seemed to find of interest was a sea of still faces on the surface of an opposite wall.   He darted his eyes around, prepared to run as if the silent images would notice him.   His attention rested on the image of a face beside the name *Talitha Coomy*.

Underneath Talitha's unmoving picture were various pieces of information – her heart beat, blood pressure, body temperature, age... Her location was also listed – currently *Education Center 35.*

The large glass panel was covered with the pictures and numbers. About a third of the images on the panel, who belonged to people whose body temperatures were over a hundred degrees, were glowing yellow. The pictures were organized by *Family Units,* and Jonah noticed that no one on the wall was wrinkled – both because most of the faces were fat, and because he could find no one older than sixty years old. A fifty-eight year old woman, alone in her family unit, was glowing with a steady red, though her vital signs were better than those whose were glowing yellow.

Jonah suddenly noticed quick, heavy footsteps behind him.

Turning, he stood face to face with a man in his thirties, who was obviously out of breath.

"What are you *doing?*" the man demanded.

Jonah's eyes widened, glancing through the blocked doorway at the distance toward the Sanitation Center entrance. He braced his legs to run.

The man moved out of Jonah's way, smacking the blinking red circle with the palm of his hand. The pulsating noise immediately ceased.

"Well?" he said, glaring at Jonah. "How long were you going to let that alarm go off? You're going to make us both lose our purpose assignments!"

"Oh," Jonah replied, releasing the breath he didn't realize he was holding. "I... I didn't know..."

"That's the whole reason you're here, isn't it?" the man interrupted. "You *were* sent from a different sector because of the sickness to relieve Aile, right?"

Jonah cleared his throat. "Er, yes."

The man crossed his right hand to his left shoulder, his fingers resting on his pudgy collarbone. "The name's Rayev."

Jonah assumed at first that he was simply scratching his shoulder, but the man's hand rested there long enough for it to seem awkward. Rayev cocked his head expectantly, continuing to hold his position. "You've got a name, don't you?"

Jonah copied the position, placing his hand across his chest. "Jonah," he responded, hoping that the motion was a greeting, and that he was not simply copying a random movement.

Rayev dropped his hand, as if to confirm the hope. "Well, if you're going to take Aile's post, then you'll need to do a better job of picking up the tasks."

"Hit the... Hit the... glowing..." Jonah fumbled as he dropped his hand, not knowing what to call the blinking red object.

Rayev squinted. "Uh, yes, hit the Resource Harvest Extension button – but only when the alarm goes off." Rayev looked at Jonah as if he were covered in chicken feathers.

"Are you from sector 20? You smell absolutely— And you look like you're wearing last week's clothes. I know sector 20 has had some delays recently, but if you knew you were coming here, you should have made sure to wear the current Fashion Committee provision. And probably sanitized yourself. I'm not trying to be insensitive."

"Sector 20, yes," Jonah said, clearing his throat again. He looked at his clothing and at those of the man in front of him.

To him, except for the fit, they looked identical.

"You're not somebody from the labor class that they're just trying to unload on us, are you?   Forefathers know we're already teeming with them here."   As he spoke, he was obviously analyzing the discrepancies on their clothing, with a bit of disdain.

"No, sir."

"Sir?" Rayev smirked.   "I can handle being called *Sir*... What was your last post?   You look young – like you should still be in the Education Center."

Jonah didn't think that 'farmer' or 'hunter' would be the kind of post that would satisfy the man's inquiry, and started clearing his throat before he even found the answer to speak.

"This is my first post, sir.   Just got out of the... Education Center."

"Figures," Rayev scoffed, "Of course the Purpose Assignment Committee wouldn't send one of their good appointees.   Wouldn't waste them on *us*."

Rayev turned around to look at the panel of glowing buttons, as if he realized that they hadn't been receiving the correct amount of attention.   "Well, get over here."

Jonah edged toward the wall, directed by Rayev's finger pointing at a mass of buttons.

"The most important thing you've got to do is just make sure that if any of these buttons go off, you hit them."

"Go off?" Jonah asked, imagining one of the circles physically falling off the wall.

"You know – if the alarm goes off, like that one that was red before," Rayev said, pointing to what was now a dull bluish circle. His voice and actions were slowly taking on more of a superior tone, as if each word that exchanged solidified his own confidence – and Jonah's lack of knowledge.

Jonah nodded his head. "What do they do?"

"Ha," Rayev chortled. "If I knew that, they'd probably appoint me to be a Technology Maintenance Officer!"

"Then why do you push them, if you don't know what they do?" Jonah asked curiously.

Rayev's forehead furrowed a bit, as if the question was unreasonable. He glanced at Jonah.

"Yes, definitely behind the times. Sector 20 must be pretty... different... eh?" he said. "You push them because you're supposed to push them. People have been sitting in this room since before you were born – since before *I* was born."

Even though Rayev was only in his thirties, he made the statement as if he were the oldest and wisest man for miles. "I guarantee you that if you *don't* push them, then it won't be too long before they appoint you to the labor class. Best not to try to cause any trouble, unless that's the type of thing that you'd prefer."

Rayev laughed.

Jonah peered closer at the buttons. He hadn't noticed previously, but there were small images on them. He didn't recognize what most of them were, but the image on the dark blue button looked like a single drop of liquid.

"How often does the alarm go off?"

"Don't tell anybody," Rayev said, lowering his voice a bit, "because this is probably one of the easiest posts in the whole Facility – but a button might go off only once or twice a month! Leaves plenty of time for killing on the digitiles or your—"

Rayev looked down at Jonah's forearm, for the first time realizing he didn't have a piece of glass wrapping around it.

"Where's your wristile?"

Jonah looked down as well, his mind blank. He glanced around the room, not knowing if it was the sort of thing he could simply find lying in the corner. "I—"

"How in the name of the Forefathers could you have forgotten it? That's not good…" Rayev shook his head. "I'll see if I can't get an extra one to you. I don't have a clue about how you could survive even an hour without it, though! The whole Facility could pass you by! What's wrong with you, Sector 20?"

Rayev turned toward the door.

"Right now?" Jonah asked, surprised that their conversation was so quickly ended.

"Of course, right now – if I didn't have my wristile on for even two minutes, I think I'd break into cold sweats! You're good here, right?" Rayev left the room before Jonah had a chance to respond.

Cold sweats, Jonah thought. *He's already sweating, and it feels like this place is stuck in a perpetual cool Autumn breeze.*

Jonah wiped his own brow, realizing he'd been tense the entire time that he had not been alone. He debated simply leaving now, so that Rayev would return to an empty room, but he didn't feel he was in danger of being discovered in his presence. Rayev seemed quick to fill any sort of silence, answering his own questions.

Since this was the first contact he had made with any of the underground population, he figured he would try to learn as much from him as he could – especially since Rayev seemed to be thrilled at being given the respect that was commonplace on the surface.

CHAPTER FIVE

During the well over three hours that passed before Rayev returned, Jonah spent a good deal of time studying the room as a whole. But most of it was spent studying Talitha's picture, memorizing her green eyes. At one point, when he glanced his fingers across her face, he noticed that a glowing green dot appeared on a nearby wall filled with blue lines. Later, when he watched as her current location moved from *Education Center 35* through various numbered hallways until ending at *Family Unit 37 (C-12),* the green dot moved along the wall. The wait seemed like only moments.

Rayev slowly jogged into the room, panting, but calmly sucking on the same glowing blue tube that Talitha's father was smoking.

"Ran the whole way," he said proudly, taking Jonah's arm and placing a cold black clasp around his forearm. "I ended up having to get this from the Technology Supply Committee, but they understood the need. Can't have a visitor thinking that we don't have enough to go around!"

Rayev blew smoke in Jonah's face, and he was surprised to find out it felt more like mist. It smelled sweet.

Jonah quietly said "Thanks," and eyed the object. Rayev watched him with suspicion for a moment, then impatiently grabbed Jonah's finger and pushed it against a button near Jonah's elbow after realizing that Jonah wasn't going to do it himself. The object suddenly pulsated with various lights.

The lights stopped with a single sentence remaining on the glass.

Identification chip not found - please retry or power up in diagnostic mode.

Rayev muttered, "That's weird," and held the button down until the words disappeared, then pushed it once more.

Again, lights danced across the glass, ending with the same sentence.

"That doesn't make any sense at all," Rayev said, scrunching his eyebrows. "I got this directly from the Technology Supply Committee! They wouldn't have given me one that hasn't been approved by the Central Facility Computer."

Jonah stared blankly at the object, unaware of what it was supposed to do. "I... I don't know."

"You know what?" Rayev barely tried to stifle laughter. "I'd bet two assignment shifts that your identification chip didn't get the upgrade we had almost a year ago." He laughed heartily, spit gathering in the corners of his mouth. "Just when you think that you know how far behind Sector 20 is, something else sneaks up on you."

Jonah smiled nervously, and cleared his throat saying "Yeah – that must be it."

Rayev held the button down on the wristile until it again was blank. He started to take it off of Jonah's arm, but hesitated.

"You know… Keep it on. When you download the upgrade to your chip - which you should definitely do soon - you can use that one until you get back to your sector. And it might be good to leave it on your arm, so that no one else recognizes that you don't have one. You'd definitely get some weird looks – even more than the looks you'll keep drawing if you don't get the current Fashion Committee's provisions soon!"

Rayev laughed again.

Though he made it seem that he was trying to save Jonah from being humiliated, it was obvious that he enjoyed pointing out what was so embarrassing about the way he looked.

But Jonah wasn't embarrassed. No one in his town had ever noticed the clothing he wore, save for a few days prior when he came home with his sleeves ripped off his arms and no satchel. Even then, it wasn't the kind of indignant look that Rayev had when his eyes poured over the differences of detail on his jumpsuit. The townspeople he grew up with were simply happy to keep warm in the winter, and keep the sun from scorching their skin in the summer.

Rayev walked over to the wall, and let his fingers slide across the surface in various patterns. As his fingertips moved, the wall changed images – quicker than Jonah's eyes could keep up. The surface ended on a series of blue lines and highlighted shapes, similar to the lines he had seen with Talitha's green dot. At the top of the wall, in large letters was *Sectors 35-40.*

"Here's the map of the next five sectors – well technically six since it includes the first of the next set. And this," he said, touching an arrow to the right as the top letters changed to *Sectors 30-35,* "is the last five sectors. You've seen a map like this, right?"

Jonah shook his head, not adding that he'd only seen a handful of maps in his lifetime – and none of them glowed.

"Of course you haven't," Rayev said, pursing his lips together, snorting a laugh. "It's as if they thought that they could send someone with no skill whatsoever to fill this purpose assignment."

Jonah thought to himself, *If all he has to do is just wait for a button to glow, and then touch it, then no, there really isn't any skill needed...*

Rayev clicked an arrow on the left, changing back to Sectors 35-40 and continued speaking. "We're here, the Fashion Committee's over here, and—" He pointed to various spots on the map, assuming that Jonah knew what all of them were for. "Do you know where you're sleeping? Do you have a Family Unit assignment for while you're here?"

Jonah simply nodded his head, thinking that his 'Family Unit assignment' would to be to slip back into the ducts that led to the surface and camp under the stars.

"Well, they're probably wondering where you are, since Aile's assignment shift ended about three hours ago. You should get going!"

Jonah recognized that the three hours that Rayev had been searching for an extra wristle started at the end of the absent button pusher's shift. When Rayev was the one who was supposed to be sitting in the room, waiting for the alarms. And in looking at the map on the wall, he could see a block labeled *Technology Supply Committee* only a corridor away. He didn't know where Rayev had been, but he got the feeling that he wasn't seeking to accomplish much during that time.

Rayev blew another puff of smoke mist that hit Jonah in the face.

"What is that?," Jonah asked.

"The flavor of Chemvapor? 'Black Resource.' Pretty great, right? Tastes like dessert!"

Rayev sat down on a chair in the corner of the room and propped up his feet. "Aile's shift starts same time again tomorrow – so if he's still sick, that's when you'll need to be here."

"Oh... Okay," Jonah said, surprised at the sudden change in Rayev. It seemed for a time that Rayev had enjoyed telling Jonah about the environment that they were in, but that time had apparently abruptly past.

Rayev picked up a contraption similar to what Talitha's brother, Dawkin, was wearing. He said with a smile, "I've got things to do, you know – these games aren't going to win themselves!" He put the hat-like object on his head, pulled a visor down, and soon after it seemed that Jonah was alone in the room.

He looked at the map, studying the path to *Family Unit 37 (C-12)* – both to try to see Talitha before leaving, and also considering that there might be a more direct way back to the system of ducts rather than going through the Sanitation Center.

But he decided that getting lost in the underground maze, as long as he were to see Talitha in person, would be worth it.

"Thanks, Rayev!" he said as he turned to leave the room. Rayev made no effort to respond, and simply continued to puff his Chemvapor in a trance.

.- .-- .- -.- .

Jonah received the occasional perplexed look from eyes that scanned his whole body, most likely noticing the invisible difference in dress, but that was the exception to the general encounter.

At first, he had walked cautiously, avoiding hallways occupied by anyone else, but he soon realized that it did not matter. Most of the people he passed by or walked behind had their attentions glued to either the glass on their forearms or over their eyes. He didn't know how people were walking with the visors over their faces – the material did not look the least bit transparent – but they took the turns of the hallways and avoided any collision with no problem.

He considered how strange the situation was: he was deep

underneath the surface of the Deathlands, surrounded by an entire society of people. He walked among aliens. Or, more accurately, he was an alien walking among a people native to a town that he could have never imagined.

On the surface, he doubted that any of these underground citizens would blend in – as he felt that he mostly did here – no matter what the clothing they wore.

Here, he was confident that no one noticed him – or no one cared.

The entire time that he walked, he had been paying attention to all of the labels next to doorways to make sure of his path. He was relieved that, once he entered an area consistently littered with Family Units, the traffic in the hallways ceased.

When Jonah was merely a few paces away from Talitha's Family Unit, he paused. He had no idea what he was going to do now that his trip was complete.

He hadn't planned far enough in advance to assume that he would need a plan once he arrived at the door. He had merely been drawn to her.

He never had a problem going to a neighbor's door with a purpose, knocking on the wooden entrance to ask to borrow a tool or a basin of flour. He'd never been anxious to go to a home and yell for a friend to come outside.

But rarely a girl's home.

And... Never like this.

The girls in his small town had taken more notice of him in the past couple of years, but he knew it was because of how he was proving himself in taking care of his family after his father's accident. It felt superficial to him that the reason they would be interested is because it was obvious that he would be responsible enough to provide. And besides that, they all seemed so normal.

But, even so, he had never simply knocked on a door to announce *I'm interested in your daughter.*

Now, so close to the only girl that had ever stolen his focus, he started pacing.

To give himself a purpose, he walked the hallway in front of the door analyzing the labels along the walls. He knew that one of them, *Maintenance Duct Entrance 37C (13)*, was familiar. It was off the main tunnel near the ladder, which would make sense considering how close to the ladder he was when he originally saw Talitha's family.

He debated abandoning the idea of seeing Talitha directly and merely retreating to the maintenance duct entrance to see if it led him to the surface. He could even traverse the tunnels before he left to watch her again.

The thought of it seemed cowardly, but reasonable.

If he had not suddenly become oblivious to his surroundings, he would have noticed that the lights in the hallways had changed from a wash of white to a dull yellow. He would have recognized a low repetitive beep. He also would have noticed that, without meaning to, he stopped directly in front of *Family Unit 37 (C-12)* and was standing still.

While thoughts still raced in his head, the panel before him quickly moved an inch inward and slid inside the wall.

A plump woman with disheveled hair, bright lips, and blue

shadows under her eyes stood in the doorway.   Jonah recognized her as Gabet, Talitha's mother.

"Can I assist you?" she asked, with a tense expression that mixed impatience with a tinge of fear.

Jonah's eyes were wide, as if he were one of the animals caught in the sights of his rifle.   He had no idea what to say.

"Can... Can I assist you?" she repeated, with a painful look on her face, indicating that she was not used to his smell.   She scanned his body and contained a smirk.

I've never seen anything as beautiful as your daughter, and I would like the chance to talk to her.

The thoughts jumbled through his head, but he did not answer her.

If you would permit me, may I take your daughter for a walk?

He was having a hard time maintaining a firm grip on the reality of the situation.

I'm from the surface, and I've watched your family through the slits in the walls.

Each option seemed worse than the last.   At last, by accident, he simply muttered, "your daughter...?"

The woman eyed him for a moment, then parted her lips in a nervous smile.   There was lipstick on her teeth.   "You're not from the Complaint Committee, are you?   Not that we have reason to complain, of course – everyone is very happy here!"

"No, ma'am, I—"

Gabet did a double take at his unfinished response and her face seemed to relax a bit, sighing.   She started to take the confrontation in consideration, noting that he was closer to her daughters age than her snap reaction. "You're looking for Talitha?"

Jonah nodded his head.

"Come in - quickly now. Give me a minute to get her..."

She darted her eyes down both directions of the hallway. The door slid behind him before Jonah realized that she had grabbed him by the arm and pulled him inside.

He was standing in the kitchen where he first observed the family. The images on the walls were the open sky, with sand and water near the floor, except for one yellow square that blinked with alert.

"Sorry to... force you like that... But there was a Facility-wide message telling us to enact protocol eleven. I honestly don't remember the last time it happened, so I had to look it up on my wristile." She laughed once, nervously, moving around the dining table toward the hallway on the opposite side of the room.

"Protocol eleven?"

"I don't think we've had to enact it since my son was in his incubation chamber. Imagine my stress then, wondering if we would ever get to bring him home because of it!

"Anyhow, it's a basic lockdown – a bit more serious than the suggested lockdowns of the protocols up through ten, but... Well, I hope not too much more serious... We haven't had any real *trouble* in the Facility since I was a little girl and there were those... What was the word? ...insurgents, I think they called them."

Jonah's body tensed up as the woman talked, knowing that he had been caught. His eyes widened, and he turned to face the door, deciding that he could possibly get away through the maintenance duct back to the surface if he left immediately.

But he had no idea where the door had gone – it was replaced with more of the same ocean scene.

After yelling "Talitha!" through the door to the hallway, Gabet chuckled to herself, noticing his anxiety. "Oh, it's nothing to worry about – I'm sure that it's nothing of the sort. I haven't heard of any problems for years. And my husband, Quilen, is on the Regulation Committee... He's sleeping from the recent sickness, and I'm sure we would've heard if it was serious.

"Honestly, it's probably just because they have fewer Control Officers available because of the sickness. I'd bet that the Central Facility Computer issued the protocol for our own safety."

As if dawn had just broken, Talitha entered the room. His anxiety waned for a moment, as if – even if he were dragged out of there – whatever would be done to him was worth seeing her up close.

The simulated ocean breeze that was pumping through the ventilation system caused strands or her hair to brush across her cheeks. She pulled it back behind her ear with one hand, the other hand holding a tattered book.

"You have a visitor," Gabet said. As she exited, she took the book out of Talitha's grip, mumbling, "I don't know why you don't just use the eyetiles to read... How many Wellness Officers have to post studies on how much better it is for your eyes for you to listen?"

Talitha's eyes followed her mother out of the room, then

glanced at Jonah. Seeing them again, Jonah realized how much more vibrant her eyes were than those from the hallways. Theirs seemed to stare blankly into glass – not caring where they stood.   Hers seemed bright with anticipation and questions, mingled with a sense that she didn't know the reason of her being here, but that she, at least, was here.

Right now, there was an obvious question in her eyes.

"Who are you?" She glanced at his clothes with confusion rather than judgment.

Jonah was silent for a moment.

"My name is Jonah..."

"I'm sorry... Have we met before?"

"No... No, we haven't met."

She looked at him as if he were alien – much in the same way that he looked at the other inhabitants of the underground facility.

"Which Committee are you with?"

"I'm not with any committee," Jonah responded.

"Are you assigned to be a Control Officer, or something? I don't know too many people as thin and muscular as you, unless they've undergone the surgeries for Control Officer appointment."

Jonah smiled briefly at the porcelain face describing him as muscular, but then realized that she wasn't saying it as a complement. "No – I'm not any of those... I... I just work."

Talitha let out the smallest noise of a gasp, looking behind her as if wondering if anyone else heard.

"You mean – you're part of the labor class? I suppose that explains why you—" She paused, holding her breath. Jonah noticed she had been taking shallow breaths, only out of her mouth, since he was close to her.

Jonah didn't know how to respond, considering that anytime he heard someone use that term it was in disdain.

"No – not exactly," he said. "You're also thin – the first I've seen here."

She eyed him suspiciously. "What do you mean the first you've seen here?"

Jonah cleared his throat. "Oh – I mean... Uh... This sector. The first I've seen in this sector."

"You're from a different sector?"

Jonah did not like lying to her. He didn't like lying to anyone – but he felt as if he was deceiving an angel when he stumbled through the words, "Sector 20."

"Oh," Talitha said, slumping her shoulders slightly. "What are you doing here?"

Jonah's body tensed, feeling like his throat would tear itself out, but calmly responded, "because of the sickness... I was sent here to help."

"No, I mean, what are you doing here. In my family's dining unit."

"I was in the hall..." Jonah's words felt like burning sandpaper. "The lockdown...and your mother..."

"Oh, I'm sorry – I thought you were here to see me since my mom called for me." She seemed slightly disappointed, while at the same time relieved. "I didn't realize that you're in here simply by coincidence."

She crossed her right arm across her chest, her fingers gracefully resting on her collarbone. "Nice to meet you, Jonah.

I'm Talitha."

Jonah mimicked her motion. "Very nice to meet you, Talitha."

There was an awkward silence while Jonah looked for something to say, and Talitha studied his expression.

"What were you reading?" he finally asked.

"Oh," she sighed, rolling her eyes slightly. "Are you going to tell me about the dangers of not using eyetiles to read, too?"

"No – I read books as well."

"They have a lot of books in Sector 20?" She pursed her lips, wondering if he was lying. He traced the contours of her face with his eyes, imagining that her lips were pressed together in preparation of a different reason.

"Uh – *ahem* – not... Not too many. I have to borrow them from a friend who collects them now that I'm out of school."

Her face softened. "Actually, I can't really talk about it – my dad wouldn't be too happy about me reading it. It's... It's not available on the eyetiles because it's not approved by the leaders. You've probably never heard of it, though, so I doubt you'd care... It's called *The Toynbee Convector*."

He locked the title away in his head, hoping that Schultz would have a copy. He wasn't great at reading, only learning enough to get him through the few written tests administered in his schoolhouse – it was a skill that never seemed to be practical. When he was still in school, the schedule was dictated by the crops. And his father often reminded him *you don't need to read to harvest corn.*

"What's it about?" he asked.

"Well," she lowered her voice. "It's actually a bunch of

different short stories, which is good because a lot of the pages are ripped out. The first one is about a man who said he built a time machine to convince people to—" She caught herself mid-thought, realizing that she didn't know who she was talking to. She finished with, "it's from a really long time ago. Before the Surface's End."

Jonah paused. It was a very strange phrase.

"What do you think happened to bring everyone down here?" he asked. "To end the surface?"

She looked at him a bit perplexed. "What do you mean? Half of our Eduction Center lectures are about why it happened."

"Right," he responded, "but don't you ever wonder what it's like up there?"

Instantly, he felt a true connection with Talitha had been made.

"All the time," she said as she looked at him, almost as he first looked at the Deathlands. Her green eyes studied his irises, as if she expected to find something hidden behind them.

"It's strange – I've never met anyone that seems to care about what's up there. I mean, between the Eduction Center lectures about the chaos of living on the surface before the Surface's End, and the leaders posting current radiation levels, I sometimes think that I'm the only one who wishes I could see it."

Jonah wanted nothing more than to tell her *I can show it to you*, but he was afraid. Afraid that she wouldn't believe him. Afraid that she *would* believe him, but not knowing how she or her family would react.

"I don't think it's as bad as they say up there."

Her face held an awkward expression. "Why do you say that?"

He hesitated, thinking of when he saw her lying down on the floor of her room through the slits in the ventilation ducts. "I... I can't tell you why, but I think that one day, you'll find out that there's just fresh air, and stars as far as you can see."

"Don't you mean *we?*" she asked, peering at him with curiosity.

"What?"

"You said one day *you'll* find out... Don't you mean one day *we'll* find out?"

"Oh," he cleared his throat. "Yes – that's what I meant."

"I'd like to think that," she continued, to Jonah's relief. "But after everything I've been told, I feel like that's kind of a hopeless thought. I'm afraid that if I actually *hope* for it, that I'll never be happy with things the way they are. At least that's what my mom always says."

"Maybe..." Jonah said. "Or maybe you're not supposed to be happy down here."

"Sector 20, you said? Maybe I'm just in the wrong sector," she sighed, as the yellow alert on the wall let out a repetitive chirp as the words changed. "We might be here for a while – can I get you anything?"

Jonah had not realized it, but he was hungry, thirsty, and had to go to the bathroom. "Yes, may I use your washroom?"

Talitha's eyebrows perked up. "Washroom?" she asked. "Do you mean the Sanitation Unit?"

Jonah said, "Yes," hoping that would direct him to the

right place.

"Happily – first door on the left," she said smirking, motioning him into the hallway behind her.

Closing the door behind him, everything in the Sanitation Unit was unfamiliar. Few in his town had indoor plumbing, but of all the washrooms he'd seen, none of them were quite as ornate as the Coomys'. Black glass lined the walls and illuminated upon his entrance, and each of the surfaces were also made of the same smooth material.

The most natural thing someone could do, and I have no idea how to do it in this room.

.- .-- .- -.- .

Some time had passed before he walked backed into the dining room and Talitha's family, minus her father, were sitting at the table eating. As he entered, only Talitha looked up.

Dawkin snickered, "Have some trouble in the Sanitation Unit? You were in there for thirty minutes!"

"Hush, Dawkin. He wasn't in there that long," Talitha snapped at her brother, who immediately went back to being engrossed in his eyetiles.

"Sorry – they're a little different in Sector 20... I couldn't figure out—" Jonah stumbled.

"Would you like to stay for dinner?" she said, immediately following up with, "well, not that you really have any other options while we're in lockdown."

"Sure," Jonah answered, making his way to the empty seat, "Thanks."

He examined the table, remembering that he'd seen the family touching it to receive their food. While part of him wanted to figure out how it worked, the other more convincing part of him did not want it to end up on a plate directly in front of him. He thought about the *Food Substance* room, and his first reactions to it.

"Your father... Your mother said he was sleeping from the sickness. Is he okay?"

"Yeah – he'll be fine. The Wellness and Pain Committee said that the cure would take a day or two."

Gabet was absent mindedly flicking at moving objects on her wristile. "Well, this is interesting," she said looking up, surprised to see Jonah at the other end of the table, having not paid attention when he walked in.

"What's interesting, mom?" Talitha asked.

"The lockdown is about to be lifted – apparently the Regulation Committee found bullets in a Sanitation Center. But there's no need to worry – they're not real bullets."

Jonah stiffened in his chair slightly. "What do you mean *not real bullets*, ma'am?"

Gabet smirked a bit. "It looks like someone was trying to recreate bullets from a long time ago, so they couldn't actually be used. The reports say that it looks like they weren't made with standard Facility synthesizing equipment – so it's probably somebody in the labor class. Still, the Facility is going to dispatch extra Control Officers just to be safe. Sounds a bit ridiculous if you ask me... Why would someone risk imprisonment to make useless pieces of metal?"

As they were speaking, the yellow panels in the wall faded into the ocean scene.

"Well," Talitha said in response to the end of the lockdown. "You can still stay for dinner, but you're free to go now." Jonah was pleased to see that she wasn't urging him to go.

Jonah looked into her green eyes, wishing he could overlook the sludge on the plates in front of the Coomys. To stay for dinner would mean eating their food, which wasn't a viable option. "Believe me, there's nothing I would like more than to stay... But, I really must be going."

Talitha's face fell slightly.

"But, do I have your permission to see you again?" he said nervously.

Her lips spread wide in reaction, then slowly formed into a subdued smile.

"Yes."

CHAPTER SIX

Jonah stood in the creek near the Deathlands at dawn, spending far more time bathing than he ever had before. He had taken a small cube of soap from the Coomy's Sanitation Unit, hoping that the next time he interacted with the citizens underground, he would not raise so many eyebrows – or noses. He had felt bad about taking the soap, but he would figure out a way to pay them back for it later.

He had almost made it up the ladder to the surface the previous evening, his mind wandering, before he remembered that he'd left his things in the Sanitation Center. He debated retrieving it, for fear that there might be Control Officers guarding it, but decided that it would be far worse if they found all of his belongings.

He planned on simply ducking into the room of buttons were there any trouble, but he found it to be completely empty. For all the sense of urgency from Gabet's relay of the Facility alert, there was no visual change, except that there were fewer people in the halls.

Letting his underground uniform dry draped over a branch, he quickly finished his breakfast of a squirrel from one of his traps.

Removing most of the contents, he placed a few pears and a handful of pecans from nearby trees into his satchel, which he hid under the extra folds of fabric of the uniform when he dressed.

He pondered not only the interactions he had with the people below the surface – mainly Talitha – but also something incredibly curious that he found when he crossed the threshold between the Deathlands and grass.

He was almost positive that when he placed the flags marking the trail to the entrance, he had started with a flag right at the threshold. However, when he exited the Deathlands the night before, the last flag was at least eight feet from the edge. There was obviously no trouble in navigating back to the grass, but he was racking his brains, trying to visualize himself placing this flag so far into the Deathlands.

In addition to that, there was a thick line of dead grass edging the threshold. Did he simply overlook that before? Had he overlooked that all the years of staring out into the expanse? He could not once remember a gradual change from Deathlands to pasture.

He reminded himself, however, it had been less than a

week ago that he chased the buck into the cracked plain. Before that, even if he had approached it, he had never crossed the line. *Perhaps the dead grass had always been there?* he thought.

It didn't matter, though. It was secondary to the thoughts surrounding Talitha.

He quickly made his way back down the shaft. After glancing through the slits into Talitha's empty room, he strolled out of *Maintenance Duct Entrance 37C (13),* passed the door to the Coomys' Family Unit, and ended up back in the room of blinking lights.

He wasn't concerned about actually standing in for Aile's assignment – apparently people in the Facility were rewarded for simply sitting in a chair for hours at a time with nothing to do – but he did feel that it would be good to keep up the appearance that he was sent to relieve the sick button pusher.

He studied the Facility maps, the faces, and the words covering the glass walls, quietly eating the fruits and nuts from inside his jumpsuit as time passed. He perked up with each change in Talitha's location, heart rate, temperature.

Rayev waddled in, again short of breath, and made an excuse about why he was late to his post – something about a Diplomacy and Sensitivity meeting because he'd pointed out that someone's hair looked unusual for the calendar. Jonah had the feeling that he was often late, and that there probably wouldn't be much of a difference if he weren't.

After saying that Jonah smelled much better today, he followed it with "Not saying you smelled bad yesterday – I'm not complaining... Forefathers know that I don't need *another*

Diplomacy and Sensitivity meeting. I'm just saying... You smell better. That's not insensitive, right?"

Before Rayev slipped on his eyetiles, he called out, "See you later, Sector 20!"

Jonah headed to Talitha's Family Unit after stopping at a Public Sanitation Unit in order to save the embarrassment of trying to use theirs without much grace.

He knocked on their door for a few minutes, when it finally slid open with Talitha standing in the entrance. "Oh – hi Jonah," she said with a shy smile. "Why didn't you use your wristile to notify us that you were outside the door? We almost always ignore the manual motion alert."

Jonah raised the arm that the lifeless glass encased. "It doesn't work – something about the different sectors and my... My chip."

"That's weird," she said as she walked through the room, motioning him to follow. She walked into her bedroom, and Jonah waited at the doorway before entering.

"What's wrong?" she asked.

Jonah hesitated.

In his home, his parents would never allow him to have a girl in his bedroom, even if his siblings were there. But his parents weren't here.

"Nothing... Nothing's wrong," he said as he took a timid step inside.

"Are you sure?" she asked with a smirk on her face. "You look like you're walking through a force field or something."

He wrestled with his thoughts of both excitement and trouble as he tried to muster a calm look on his face. "Your...

Your parents don't mind if I'm in here with you?"

She laughed a bit, as if he were joking, then noted his stony expression. "Of course they don't mind – why would they?"

"I just... I didn't know if—" He stopped himself, not wanting to make the situation even more awkward. His heart was thumping loudly in his ears. "Never mind."

"You're sure you're from Sector 20?" she asked, smiling. "I wouldn't expect that only seventeen sectors away, there would be so many differences in the way we live."

"More than you'd believe."

"Tell me about it, then," she said, sitting on the edge of the bed. "Tell me about your sector."

He moved to a chair at the opposite side of the room, walking softly as if the room itself were sacred. If his mother and father knew that he was alone with a girl in her bedroom, they would not be very pleased. Of course, they probably would not have been pleased that he had been watching her through the slits in the walls, either. He couldn't seem to stop himself from breaking what he considered to be obvious rules – especially when this didn't seem to be strange to her at all.

"Where should I begin?" he asked as he eased into the chair uncomfortably.

"I don't know – what are things like there? What is your purpose assignment? Do you have a brother or a sister? Any of that."

"Well, yes, I have a brother and a sister – Harrison is eleven and Lillian is thirteen. I guess you'd say that—"

"Wait – you have a brother *and* a sister?" The perplexed look crossed her face again. Jonah noticed that she often held that expression when he answered questions.

"Yes," he answered, "I'm the oldest, then Lillian, then Harrison."

"I thought the limit was two children per Family Unit across the whole Facility?"

"Oh – uh... I don't know," he stammered. Almost all of the families in the village had more children than two children. "There are a few families that only have one child, so maybe they're not as strict where I am?"

It wasn't a lie – there were a few families in the village that only had one child, but it was fairly rare, and generally because they weren't able to have more. Most families around the small town had at least five children, with the expectation that they'd share the workload once they were old enough.

"I should start writing this stuff down," Talitha laughed. "The Regulation Committee isn't as strict on family size, your Identification Chip doesn't work with our wristles, you call your Sanitation Units – what was it? Washers?"

"Uh... Washrooms."

"You've asked my permission to come into my room, and if you could see me again... Your skin isn't pale but I don't think you're of a different melanin shade... You said you're muscular because of work, but that you're not part of the labor class... None of that was supposed to be insensitive – I've just never met anyone like you."

"I've... I've never met anyone like you either," Jonah breathed.

"So – you said that you're not part of the labor class... What did you say your purpose assignment is?"

Jonah thought hard to his conversations with Rayev. In none of them had Rayev used terms to describe what the job was called. "I'm here to stand in for someone named Aile," he coughed. "I push buttons when alarms sound."

"You're a Resource Officer?" she said, leading him.

"Yes – a Resource Officer."

"It doesn't sound like you know much about it – what do you do while you're in Sector 20?"

Jonah thought about the last seventeen years of his life, farming and hunting with his family. Technically, he thought, all of his time was spent gathering and maintaining resources. If that was the equivalent of sitting in a glowing room, pushing buttons that chirp, then he wasn't proud of the position, but at least there was a name for it.

"I am a Resource Officer there as well."

"I'm sorry, but that doesn't make any sense," Talitha accused. "Yesterday, when I asked why you were thin, you said you *worked*. As far as I understand, Resource Officers have one of the easiest jobs in the whole Facility. My brother wants to be a Resource Officer because he wants to play games on his eyetiles all day."

"It's different where I'm from," he said, worried that more questions would doom him. "What about you – you're thin and beaut... Er..." He blushed, as did she. "What do you do differently from everyone else here?"

Talitha's aggressive posture had melted a bit because of being (almost) called beautiful, and she had a sheepish grin on her face.

"I think... I think I'm just the only person that cares," she said. "Everyone eats until they're sick, and stares at tiles all day – wristiles, eyetiles, digitiles... I *walk* to the Education Center rather than riding a Magnet Cart. I'm not satisfied with eating a bunch of dessert. I just... I just want something more than everyone else here seems to."

Jonah felt sorry for her. She was a bird in a cage, unaware that the door was unlocked. He felt that by not showing her the surface, he was condemning her to a prison that confined her with so many others that were too easily satisfied. But he was still afraid.

He looked at the sadness in her eyes and felt that he could at least dip his toe in the waters of what might be irresponsibility.

"Have you ever heard of pecans?" he asked.

She shook her head, her gaze on the floor.

Jonah turned his body away from her and awkwardly reached down into the satchel under his uniform. Pulling out two pecans that remained, he turned back around and reached them out to her.

She looked up and asked, "What is that?"

"Pecans."

"What is pecans?"

"Pecans are nuts. They're food."

Her eyes widened.

"I didn't know they made them – nuts have been outlawed for over a hundred years!" She abruptly stood up, whispering, "if somebody finds out that you broke into one of the Resource Centers and stole unprocessed food substance, you could be reassigned to the labor class, or worse! How do you know that you're not already contaminated by them?"

"I didn't steal them," he assured her, his heart racing from watching the panic in her eyes. "And what do you mean contaminated by them?"

"How else would you get them? You said that you're a Resource Officer – is that how you *work*? You sneak into the Resource Centers and steal unprocessed food substance?"

"No!" Jonah forced out in a steady breath, looking out the door to make sure no one was nearby. "I promise – I didn't steal them. These are not from the Resource Center."

"How do you explain them, then?" she said in heavy breaths, keeping her voice low. "It's illegal to try to make any private resources. My dad would be the first to call the Control Officers if he saw those."

Jonah didn't know how to recover. The simple act that he hoped would give her a glimpse of hope had turned him into a thief in her eyes. "Like I said – it's different where I'm from."

"So nobody in Sector 20 pays attention to the Regulation Committee, is that what you're saying?"

He watched her pace for a moment in front of him. "Please sit down," he said.

She hesitated, but sat down after staring at him.

"Something isn't right about you, Jonah. Sorry – I'm not complaining or trying to be insensitive... But there are so many differences, and I can't imagine that it's just because you're from a different sector. I keep bracing myself for you to say that you're from the future, or the past or something, like *The Toynbee Convector*."

Jonah's heart calmed as her voice smoothed. "What did

you mean, asking if I was contaminated by them?"

"You should have paid more attention in Pseudo Modern Food Substance lectures... I know it's required - I had it about three years ago. There were a number of things that they kept as individual food substances – like nuts – because a few of the Facility's children population would get sick, and even die if they ate them. One time, someone gave a certain nut food substance – I think nut substance P – to a leader's child. The child died, and the leader went on to make all of the individual food substances illegal."

Jonah tilted his head. "If only a few people could get hurt by them, why would they make them illegal for everyone? Why wouldn't people just take the responsibility of keeping their kids, or themselves, away from it?"

"Actually, I remember one of his speeches from the lecture: 'if P nut substance has the possibility of killing even one more child, why would we allow anyone to consume it?'"

Jonah shook his head. "What if they keep finding things that hurt only one person? What will they do with that new food?"

"Oh, they do all the time," Talitha responded. "They ban a new individual food substance at least once a year. If a person falls ill, the Wellness and Pain Management Committee breaks down the food substance that they ate to determine which ingredient made them sick. They usually can replace it with a similar synthetic, and no one knows the difference. They've been working extra lately because of the number of people that started getting sick a couple days ago."

"Do *you* know how the food substance is made?" Jonah

asked, wondering if everyone in the Facility knew about the cages in the Resource Center.

"Almost everything is synthetic now – a long time ago people would put things in dirt in order to eat it. Or they would raise a species from birth just to eat it. I have to admit, it seems a little gross if you ask me. I can't understand how they did it – how they would have been able to create food substance without the technology we have now, but I guess that's something we'll never know."

Jonah thought again about the cages, and then his own farm. She had no idea how food was *supposed* to taste. "Would you like to try this pecan, or am I going to eat them both myself?"

There was a long, awkward pause.

"I've never eaten anything but the regulated food substance... How do you know it's safe to eat something unprocessed - especially nut food substance?"

He grabbed one of the pieces of the nuts that had already been cracked open. He popped it in his mouth and chewed. "I've been eating them all morning," he said. After a moment, he sat back down in the chair.

Talitha looked away and held out her hand. He walked over to her and placed the pieces in her hand, lingering when he touched her skin.

After seeing no sign that Jonah was falling ill, Talitha slowly, cautiously, put a small piece of pecan in her mouth and swallowed.

She immediately began to gag, coughing violently. "I'm contaminated!!" she gasped for air as her shoulders shook.

"You're supposed to chew it first!" Jonah cried. He ran to her side, not knowing what to do.

"Fluid!" she coughed.

Jonah looked around for a faucet of some sort – the only one he remembered being the one in the Sanitation Unit – so he ran to grab some water from the tap. He frantically looked around for a cup, but found nothing.

Running back into Talitha's room, he found her drinking from a tube protruding from the wall. Her coughing had ceased.

"Where did you go?" she asked, still trying to clear her throat. "Were you trying to kill me?"

"I went to get you some water, but I didn't know how to bring it back in here," Jonah reasoned.

"From the *Sanitation Unit*??"

"I... I didn't know how else to get water."

She held up the tube from the wall. "I couldn't expect you to know how to get a normal fluid tube from the digitiles," she coughed again. "I guess you drink Sanitation Unit water in Sector 20."

She slammed the remaining pieces of pecan onto the table beside her bed. "I think I'll refrain from trying to kill myself today."

"Sorry," he apologized. "I assumed you'd know to chew it up before you swallowed it."

"That's not how we eat in Sector 37," she said as she took another drink. "That's not how anyone in the Facility eats."

She furrowed her brow.

"Ok," she said, "I'm serious. What is with you?"

"What do you mean," Jonah tried to respond innocently.

"I mean, if you don't tell me what is going on – why you are so *weird*, and why you tried to kill me with unprocessed food – then you're going to have to leave."

Jonah sat stone cold for a moment, not knowing what to do. He obviously wasn't a good enough liar to keep her in the dark, and he definitely didn't want to be thrown out of her home.

"You..." he started. "You wouldn't believe me."

"I'm pretty sure I don't believe you now," she said, "so I doubt you can surprise me."

Jonah took a deep breath and slowly let it out.

"I'm not from here."

Talitha was not satisfied.

"Yes, I think we've established that," she responded. "From where, then? And don't tell me Sector 20."

"From..." Jonah didn't know if his next words would get him thrown out, thrown into some sort of jail, or thrown into the arms of the girl sitting in front of him.

"From up there."

He pointed at the ceiling of the room.

She looked up, then back down in his eyes. Her eyes were narrow.

"Like, you live in some secret level above this one?"

"Not quite," Jonah breathed. "I live on the surface."

Talitha was silent for a moment.

"Oh, I understand now," she said, as if she had a revelation and connected all the dots in her head. "*That's* why you brought unprocessed food. And you wanted me to drink *water.*" The level of sarcasm slowly rose in her voice, and ended in an obvious tone. "*And* why your chip isn't functional, and why you say that you *work*, and why you're thin and your skin is tan."

She ended her rant by running her fingers across his face, as if expecting the color of his skin to come off.

Jonah sat helpless.

"Did Dawkin set this up? Well, very *funny* Dawkin!" she yelled, moving toward the door. "You got me – I look like a moron!"

Jonah stood with his open palms out to Talitha, wide-eyed. "Shhh... Please don't say anything," he pleaded.

"You know, Jonah," she said, turning back around towards him. "I actually liked you. Even with your quirks. You're one of the first people in my life that seemed like more than just some... some robot. But you're just here to make fun of the unhappy girl. To ridicule me for wondering what it was like before the Surface's End. To make a big joke out of the fact that I think stars are pretty, and that I'm jealous of the people that were able to see them without their skin burning off. Well, great job. Ha. Ha. *Ha.*"

She turned away from him, pursing her lips.

Her mother came into the doorway, flustered. "What's all this commotion about? Talitha, are you trying to make a fool of yourself in front of your guest?"

"No," Talitha said. "Jonah was just leaving. And I'm not the one trying to make a fool of me."

"But," Jonah protested. "I'm not trying to make a fool of you. I'm trying to—"

"Mom – would you show Jonah out?"

Jonah looked over at Gabet's confused eyes surrounded in blue, and realized that it was not the time to try to redeem himself with the truth. If Talitha wouldn't listen, then her parents definitely wouldn't.

"Well, it looks like it's time to go," Gabet said to him with a steady tone.

Jonah walked through the Coomy's Family Unit. As they approached the door, Gabet whispered, "Sorry about Talitha – she can get a bit – excited – about things... I'm sure she'll be fine in a few days. Of course, I guess you'll be back to your sector, since everything will be back to normal by then!"

She seemed a bit too happy in relation to Jonah's distress.

When the door closed behind him, he made his way back through the ducts, and found himself at the slits in Talitha's wall.

Stars shown all over her room, and she lay face down on her bed, sobs muffled in her sheets.

.- .-- .- -.- .

Jonah awoke in his own bed, tiptoeing out of the room to get to his normal morning routine. It had been days since his return, and he tried to keep to himself more than usual. His family was simply trying to help when they realized that he seemed depressed, but this time he spent his time dodging their questions.

His father found him in the middle of their cornfield – which took a decent amount of effort on a lame leg, so Jonah felt that the least he could do was talk.

"When'd you meet her?" Thomas asked, after nearly catching his breath.

"What?" Jonah shot back, a bit too surprised.

"Bud, you've been moping around here for the past couple of days. Before that it seemed like you couldn't get back to the hunt fast enough – or wherever you were trying to go. I don't know of too many things that can change a man's mood that fast."

Jonah avoided eye contact with his father and continued picking ears of corn off the stalks. "It doesn't necessarily mean it's a girl," he said.

"True," Thomas said, leaning on his crutch. "Go ahead and tell me about the non-girl-related situation, then."

Jonah worked in silence for a few seconds.

"It doesn't necessarily mean it's not a girl, either," he finally admitted.

Jonah's dad smirked.

"Well," Jonah said, pausing. "I saw her during my last hunting trip... From another town." He technically hadn't seen Talitha on the trip that he killed the buck, but at this point his fascination with the object in the Deathlands was overtaken with his fascination with her.

His father nodded knowingly, still smiling.

Jonah continued, "and I met her this last trip out... But I don't think she wants to see me again."

When Jonah offered nothing more, Thomas said, "I

remember the first time I saw your mother. That woman took my breath away."

"Dad," Jonah said, "you and mom grew up together... I doubt that playing leap frog at four years old is quite the same."

"I used to be quite the leap frogger," Thomas quipped. "Don't think I could keep up these days," he said, patting his cane.

"But, no, that's not what I meant. The first time I really *saw* her."

He wiped the sweat from his forehead and continued, "I guess I was about your age, and I was gone for a summer to help Doc Thorton's uncle with his crops a town over. All of his kids got sick, and two of them ended up not making it, so the doc and I went out there to try to take care of things when he was in bad shape. That's actually the reason that Doc got interested in medicine – he was pretty close to one of his cousins that died and he didn't want to lose anybody like that again.

"That was a hard summer. The doc ended up spending most of his time trying to get his other cousins well – reading a bunch of old books and what-not – and I did everything I could not to let them lose any of their crops, as if that meant anything compared. Working from sun up to sun down, and then canning everything I could 'til I pretty much collapsed into bed.

"When my work was done and all the crop was in, I hopped on my horse and rode back to town by myself, feeling like I hadn't had a good night's sleep in a few months. All I could think about was your grandma Whitfield's cooking and a little bit of hibernating.

"But I saw her at the edge of town, standing up at the top of Miller's hill picking flowers. Lord, I still remember how the wind was blowing her red hair in her face. She'd just keep brushing it back. Looked like the sun was shining just for her – like if she walked away it would've been the middle of the night.

"I led my horse to the pond at the bottom of the hill, and just sat there staring at her for forever. I think she must've liked the attention, because she kept picking the same dang flowers," Thomas smiled, lost in nostalgia.

"Truth be told, I barely even recognized her. Before I left that summer, she was just a girl that I'd seen on the playground – but when I came back... Heck, it took me two days before I got up the nerve to kind of re-introduce myself. And when I did, I stammered all over the place.

"I thought I came back to town to get a little rest, and get back to my normal life – but I didn't get much sleep after that. Her daddy would have to shoo me off their front porch every night, and I'd work faster than ever so my daddy would let me go so I have a little more time with her."

Thomas stared off into space for a minute, reliving memories. "And I'm the luckiest man alive now – I don't have to get shooed off the front porch anymore. I get to brush the hair out of her face when I wake up every morning."

Jonah realized that he had stopped picking corn while his father spoke, and he started back up again.

"I know I seem like an old man to you, Jonah," Thomas said. "But to tell you the truth, I don't think that forty is very old. And if it weren't for my leg, I think I'd still feel like I was twenty. I remember what it felt like to be scared of having your mom tell me that she could never love me. To tell me that she couldn't see me as anything but a boy that used tease her or reject her to go play with the boys.

"And I hate to spoil the surprise ending, but despite the fear, I realized it was worth putting myself on the line. The worst thing that could happen is that I was right... That she didn't care about me, and I would have my heart broken. But, if that were the case, at least I would've known it for sure and I could stop wondering and being afraid. But – the best thing that could happen is what happened. And all this - even you kids - couldn't have happened if I hadn't risked it."

Jonah took a deep breath and looked at his dad. "But what if it's the first option? What if she really doesn't want to see me anymore?"

"Well," Thomas said, scanning the cornfield and letting out a small chuckle. "If that's the case, I guess you can go ahead and keep being depressed, after you know that for sure."

But what if she says no, and I get thrown in some sort of a jail in the Facility? Jonah wanted to ask. Instead, he just said, "Thanks, Dad."

"Welcome, bud," Thomas said as he started walking out of the field, every other step a little slower. "And you know what I found out later? Your mom hurried to finish her chores just so she could pick the same flowers at Miller's hill every day that summer. She'd been waiting for me to notice her long before then."

CHAPTER SEVEN

Jonah changed into the Facility uniform that he stashed in
the tree after bathing in the creek and the morning sun.

He had realized his dad was right, and that he'd rather he
- and Talitha - knew the truth than wonder for the rest of his
life. When he was about to leave his home again, his mother
had probed so intensely that his father made up a story about
sending Jonah to another town for some supplies. After she
pressed even more, asking what supplies the other town had
that wasn't available nearby, his father told her that Jonah held
the family's load on his shoulders for a long time; that if Jonah
wanted to go, he had more than earned it.

He pedaled his bike into the Deathlands. Seeing the first
flag he placed well within the boundaries of the gray ground,

he was positive that either the flag had moved even further –
or that the Deathlands had. The ring of dead grass was gone.

He arrived at the Coomy's door, and Talitha's mother
finally opened it after he waived his arms and knocked for a
while.

"Oh – hello!" Gabet said, surprised. "Are you still here? I
assumed that you went back to your sector?"

"Uh... I did," Jonah said, clearing his throat. But I came
back to see Talitha."

Gabet smiled and moved out of the doorway. "Come in,
then. She's in her room. You're so nice for coming back –
hopefully she won't have another outburst."

"Thanks," Jonah said as he walked past her.

"By the way," she said as he crossed the room, "use your
wristile to notify us that you're outside next time. We almost
never pay attention to the manual motion alert. And you
might want to check in with the Fashion Committee."

"Yes, ma'am," he responded as he left the room.

He knocked on Talitha's doorframe, and she looked up,
sitting on the floor.

"Hi," he said sheepishly.

"Hi," she said, looking back down at the book in her lap.

"Can I come in?" he asked.

Talitha paused, shrugged her shoulders, and motioned her
hand toward the chair. It wasn't the glowing reception he'd
hoped for, but he sat down.

"I figured you would've gone back to your sector now that
everyone is well again. Or was that part of the charade?"

Jonah pulled out a handful of flowers that he'd gathered on

the surface and laid them down in front of her.

"Do you think that flowers will make me forget about what you did?" she asked, barely noticing them. "I still don't know who put you up to it – Dawkins hasn't said anything, and he would've been rubbing it in every possible moment if it was him."

"You've seen flowers before?" Jonah asked.

"Of course I've seen flowers before – look at my desk."

He turned his head a bit and reached out to the vase containing a bouquet of lifeless fabric flowers. He pulled one close to his nose and smelled the synthetic perfume that was contained in its stem. Placing it back in the vase, he said, "Smell one of those." He pointed to the flowers on the ground.

She looked up at him. "I suppose these are *real* flowers from the surface, right?"

He nodded.

"This isn't funny to me, Jonah."

His heart sank.

"It isn't funny to me, either."

She stood, disregarding the flowers, and pressed her fingers against the surface of the glassy wall. Immediately, the boundaries of the room were covered in a beautiful meadow with countless flowers. "That's the year 2104," she said with a cold voice.

"And this," she continued while touching the wall again, "is today."

Immediately, the screens turned gray. Fires burned in the distance and ash rained all around the walls. No matter where he looked, the image remained the same. The picture disappeared and she sat back down in the floor after tossing the flowers on her bedside table.

"Flowers have been extinct for hundreds of years," she said. "They weren't found to have any necessary qualities, so the leaders of the time decided to ban them rather than waste water on them. Is that your real job? You're part of the Synthetic Committee, and have access to the computers that can make things like fake flowers and nuts?"

"Talitha... If you would come with me to the surface, I could show you—"

"So I can walk into some trap where there will be a housing unit full of people laughing at me, the unhappy girl who wishes she was on the surface? No thanks."

"How can I prove to you that I'm not lying?"

"Not lying about the surface, or about being from Sector 20?"

"Ok... Sorry... Sorry about the Sector 20 thing," Jonah said looking down. "I knew you wouldn't believe me. A man named Rayev was telling me I looked like I was from Sector 20, and so I figured that was the only way I could... I didn't think I should tell you the truth at first."

"Come with me," she said, standing up and walking out of her room. He followed.

"Mom, I'm taking Jonah to see our Sector's Education Center," she called out. He heard no response, but they walked out of the Family Unit.

The Education Center was similar to the rooms in the Coomy's home. They made their way into a small, dark, circular room that, when the door closed behind them, looked as if it had no exits. There was a bench in the center of the floor.

Talitha touched the wall, then her wristile, and sat on the bench. She motioned Jonah to sit beside her, and he did.

She showed various scenes of the outdoors pre- and post-Surface's End by controlling the walls by touching the glass surface on her arm.

"These look like the same images as the walls of your room... Why did we come here?" Jonah asked.

Talitha frowned indignantly, as if he'd asked an obvious question that he already knew the answer to. "The wall tiles in each Family Unit can only access a small amount of the Central Facility Computer's information. We can access far more here."

"So this room has all of your information? Every bit of your knowledge is on these walls?"

Talitha's furrowed brow rose as she let out a little chuckle. "You sure are good about not breaking character, Jonah. This is just our sector's Education Center."

"So this is like your schoolhouse?"

"Sure, if you'd like to call it that," she responded. "This is one of the Sensory Theater rooms where all the classes come to experience a bit of what life is and was like on the surface. Our Educators can control scents and temperature, but you have to have access from the Education Committee to do that. Anyone with a wristile can change the video and sound, though," she said, letting her hand curiously slip over the dark glass on his wrist.

"What do they let you smell, then?" Jonah asked, gulping.

"What temperature do they say it is on the surface?"

"Don't act like you haven't sat in on the lectures about the Surface's End," she said, quickly pulling her hand away from his wrist and placing it on her own wristile. "It's hot. It smells awful. They never set it to the actual temperature, though, of course – otherwise we'd all die. There's nothing like it anywhere else. The Lecturers always describe it as *burning sulfur*, as if any of us are supposed to know what that means. The Educators never let it last long, because some of the kids inevitably get sick or pass out or something."

"Hmmh," Jonah sighed. "Brother Philip, our preacher, talks about burning sulfur. I don't think I've ever heard anyone talk about it except for him, and he's always using it to describe hell!" He laughed just a bit, wondering if whoever was trying to convince everyone that the surface was unsafe was taking a page out of the book of Revelation.

"Preacher? What's that?"

"Oh, you know," Jonah responded. "He's like one of your Educators, but he only really teaches about Jesus and the Bible."

Talitha's eyes widened. "You've read the Bible?"

"Of course," Jonah said. "Er, at least some of it. It's one of the few books my family owns... It's been in our family for—"

Talitha cut him off.

"The Bible is one of the first books that was banned. I've looked for one, and as far as I can tell there hasn't been one in existence for at least three hundred years."

"So that's what will convince you, eh?" Jonah smiled. "I'm

sure Brother Philip will be excited to give a Bible to someone who has never seen one. All I need to do is bring you one, and you'll believe me?"

"I've seen *these* images since I was a little girl," she said motioning to the pictures moving on the walls. "Why do you think that I would be so gullible? If you can synthesize individual Food Substances and flowers, you could make a book."

"I'm not trying to fool you," Jonah said. "I've seen the surface differently all my life. Not hot, burning sulfur. I see a surface that is alive and fresh; a place where food and water spring up out of the ground."

"Out of the ground – like dirt, right?" she said, not truly listening. Pointing to the walls, she said "Show me."

"I don't know how... I can only show you by taking you there."

"How did you get here, then? Where did you come from? I mean – what doors and paths?"

"I came in through Surface Duct 37C."

She tapped on her wristile, and the walls of the room changed to the image of snowy gray. "That's where you came from?" she asked sarcastically.

"No," he answered, looking curiously at the moving pictures.

"Well, that's the Surface Duct that you mentioned – they're all recording video into the Central Facility Computer at all times."

"Will you go there with me?" he asked.

"I'm still... I'm still not ready to trust that you aren't just setting me up to laugh at me," she said sadly.

"Well then, show me what they showed you," Jonah said. "Instead of me trying to convince you, let me see how they convinced you of the Surface's End, and why no one has attempted to leave the Facility."

"Oh, crazy people have tried," she laughed. "Criminals, usually. People who are on the run from the Control Officers, or have defied the Regulation Committee so badly that they'd rather take the chance on the surface, I guess. They've all died trying..." Talitha's expression morphed into disgust. "...and the Regulation Committee circulates images of their burned bodies. To show us how the Facility protects us."

Jonah narrowed his eyes.

"Well, show me something to convince me that I'm wrong – that there's no way I could be from the surface."

Talitha tapped on her wristile, and a moment later the wall in front of them was filled with books. The edges of the picture ended abruptly into walls that had turned blank. From the corner of one of the walls, a man walked out wearing a dark suit. The suit was more like the clothes that he might see on the men of his town at chapel than anyone in the Facility, but much nicer. As if someone from the Facility had seen the townspeople's Sunday best and decided to improve upon it.

"Hello children!" the man beamed as he moved to the center of the picture. "I'm so excited to get to teach you about the Surface today!" He moved his hands superficially, as if preparing to take a bow. "I'm Mr. Adams."

"This is the first lecture in the series on the Surface's End," Talitha whispered. "We see it when we're much younger." She rolled her eyes, adding, "but you knew that."

Jonah thought about defending himself, but kept quiet in order to hear the speech emanating from somewhere in the walls.

"You know, I'll bet some of you ask your parents a lot of questions!   Probably questions like 'Where does Food Substance come from?' and 'How does the door know to open when I want it to?' Well – those are great questions, and we're going to spend time talking about things like that! In fact, the place we live – The Facility – takes care of a great many things, and I am happy to say that I helped build it! In order to talk about this wonderful Facility, we look back in time. All the way to the year 2104.

"Actually, that's not that long ago for me – right now it's just the year 2109 – but it might be much later than that when you're watching this! In 2104, there were some scary things going on outside of the Facility."

As he spoke, moving images appeared on the wall around his head. The images were of children crying, of people fighting, and of crowds yelling. Mr. Adams motioned his hands in the directions of the pictures.

"It might sound strange, but before we lived here, many children didn't have homes, or families, or even food to eat. The Leaders knew of all the bad things that were happening, so we came together and built this place to protect you! We made sure that you would always have full tummies and warm beds."

The negative images were replaced with families embracing, sleeping babies, and children with toothy grins eating Food Substance that had more color and texture than what he saw on the Coomys' plates.

"We realized that people weren't able to take care of themselves on their own, so we started building a wonderful home all the way underground, away from the scary parts of the world. We knew that if everyone came together and worked really hard, the Leaders would be able to make sure that everyone could have everything they needed."

The video skipped with a motion of Talitha's hand, and she whispered, "Maybe that's a little too early."

The man was again in a room full of books, but had a different color suit on.

"...but the poverty was severe," Mr. Adams continued with a slightly sterner voice, images of riots surrounding him. "Some of the wealthiest citizens were exploiting the poorest citizens, making them work in these horrible conditions. The Leaders, at that time called the *Government*, put regulations on the wealthy in order to end the exploitation, but many of them closed their factories instead of simply abiding by the new laws. The Government imprisoned many of these men and women for abandoning their employees, but the economic collapse was hastening."

Another flick of Talitha's fingers, and the man was wearing another suit and had white streaks in his hair. Pictures of machines moving dirt surrounded him.

"...acquired almost forty million acres, or a hundred and sixty billion square meters, of land beneath the surface to build the Facility. Much of it was donated, but many of the wealthiest land owners actually demanded to be *compensated* for their land. This is, of course, despite the fact that the Leaders were the rightful owners of the land, which the occupants acknowledged by paying taxes – or usage fees – on all property. This was *also* despite the fact that since the Facility was being built underground, the surface was barely changing.

"We designed the Facility to harvest many natural resources – drawing water from water tables, harvesting minerals from the surrounding ground, and created thermoelectricity by drilling deep into the earth. These property owners were claiming that they *owned* the resources on their land, and were selfishly fighting to deprive the future citizens of the Facility of these resources. These fights continued until the Surface's End.

"The social unrest was continuing, and the Leaders pooled more and more resources in order to finish the Facility before any major disaster struck. Over the decade of construction, as they completed Sectors, the Family Units were being filled with families of the most beloved citizens of the time, including social activists, celebrities, and the Leaders themselves."

Mr. Adams paused, his eyes darting to the side for a moment.

"Umm...," he continued, "It might be necessary to note that the word *celebrities* denoted someone who, at the time, was well-known and seen as perhaps more important than others. They were private citizens who were artists, musicians, or actors, and who were generally compensated much more than their peers, though their work had the same merit. After the Surface's End, the idea of the celebrity was lost over time, since the compensation of resources was equalized. Also, the Regulation Committee prohibited individuals from profiting off of others, so the arts were realized to be a waste of energy by most."

Another flick, another suit. Mr. Adams had visibly aged, but still seemed just as energetic with his gestures. His hair obviously had been dyed to his younger self's color.

"...and almost as soon as the Facility had been filled, violence on the surface turned into an all out war. When enemies found out about the Facility they started attacking nearby sites, and the Leaders made a unanimous decision to seal all entrances, and within a week the radiation levels on the surface had gone up ten fold. Miraculously, the cameras we had set up at each surface duct were still working. Unfortunately, the images that they projected were of a scorched earth. The fires that started those three decades ago are still burning today. Our hope is that one day they will cease. But our trust is that the Facility will sustain us until they do."

Talitha touched her wristile, and the gray snow surrounded them once again.

"That's definitely a vague overview, but that's the general idea," she said, as if all doubts of the Surface's End were erased.

Jonah continued to stare at the moving pictures.

"I don't understand," he said.

"What do you mean, you don't understand? Mr. Adams explained—"

Jonah cut her off.

"I know Mr. Adams explained it, and I understand what

he was saying. For the most part."

He paused.

"Before you started the lectures, you were going back and forth between images of before the end and then after... Don't you find it strange?"

"Don't I find what strange?" she asked.

"Well – he spoke of attacks. Of a war, even," Jonah said, continuing to stare at the depressing animated walls. "If there was a war, wouldn't those images show it? Especially since he showed so many violent images while he spoke?"

Talitha sat still for a moment. Then she touched her wristile, saying, "Well, then, let's find the moment right before the entrances were sealed."

After the screen jerked to a similar gray scene, the debris moved quickly in reverse. The motion sped up as she slid her finger across the glass on her arm.

The screen went black for a moment then a beautiful meadow appeared, still quickly animating in reverse.

"Just a minute," Talitha said, touching the glass.

The images moved forward slowly, then the wall turned black, save for white letters.

Classified: Central Facility Computer Archives

"Hmm... That's odd – I've never seen that message before," she admitted.

"And what about the people entering the Facility?" Jonah continued. "Is there an image of them?"

Talitha navigated the walls to a main Facility entrance not long before it was sealed. A smiling couple holding black bags walked towards an open door guarded by a man in a uniform.

Behind the couple was a family of four, their toddler scooping up dirt with his parents' approval. The scene was silent.

Talitha sped up the happy procession, families rushing toward the entrance, and ended at the same classified black screen.

She rubbed her eyes and stared at her wristile. Jonah assumed that it volunteered information, but he waited for her to announce it.

"Where's the unrest?" she finally asked. "The fear?"

She looked at Jonah as if, for the first time, he might actually know something she didn't.

He simply shrugged.

After a moment of pause, Talitha went back to her wristile. She repeatedly looked up to see the same *Classified* message.

"What are you looking for now?" Jonah asked after some time.

"Well – at first I was just trying to find other cameras from the same moment as when the first camera was classified, and they all are... Now I'm trying to find some of Mr. Adams later lectures – after the ones that they showed us in school – that might talk more about the war that ensued... But they're all classified too. It doesn't make any sense! Why would they classify Education Lectures?"

They sat for a moment staring at white letters lighting the room.

"Jonah?" she asked, breaking the silence.

"Yes?"

"Would you go with me to the Central Facility Computer? I mean, if you really want to convince me that you're not lying about the Surface. If we're there, we should be able to see some of the archived footage."

"Yes!" Jonah shouted. "Where is it?"

.- .-- .- -.- .

The Magnet Tram, in Jonah's eyes, seemed to be another strange magical contraption.

Multiple metal cubes only slightly larger than his bicycle trailer seemed to be suspended in midair. They moved quickly to a short line of people, and would pause mid-air. Each time a cube arrived, a single person would exit the box through an opening that suddenly appeared, and then a single person would enter from the line. As soon as the exchange occurred, the cube would silently zoom away, never touching the ground or the walls.

When Jonah and Talitha climbed into a cube, he realized that most of the Facility's population were riding one per cube because of how little room there was. Even the two of them were a bit cramped – though he didn't mind – and he couldn't imagine that more than one of the average large underground citizens would fit at all.

Talitha touched the glass wall inside the cube then touched her wrist. With a momentary jolt the Magnet Tram was moving at incredible speeds, though it felt to Jonah that they were sitting completely still.

"Let's just say that you're really who you say you are,"

Talitha said, breaking the silence of the speeding Magnet Tram. "And I'm not saying I believe you. But – you're not a Resource Officer. What do you do?"

"I'm a farmer and a hunter," Jonah said.

"And what exactly does a farmer and a hunter do?"

"Well, it's actually hard to explain to someone who has never eaten anything more than the Facility's Food Substance," he said, a bit perplexed. "I work with the dirt, and with water, and with animals. I make sure things grow so that my family can eat."

"What do you mean, you make sure things *grow*? Aren't there machines that control your food supply?"

"No – my family's hands control the food supply," he said, picturing the metal contraptions that moved the animal cages in the Resource Center. He assumed those were the *machines* she referred to. "If we don't work, we don't eat. And pardon me for saying so, but I'd never trust one of those *machines* to take care of what I put in my stomach."

"What do you mean?" she said with a blank stare. "I've seen the lecture videos of Food Substance being made. I don't see how human hands could keep the raw materials so clean. And the Lecturers have said that the way the Facility produces Food Substance is better than methods used before the Surface's End."

"So you've seen the cages, and the animals with liquids being pumped into them?" Jonah asked, sad that she knew how the animals were treated.

"Gross," Talitha winced. "They don't use real animals - Food Substance is made of synthetics. Do you expect me to believe you'd rather have a dead creature for dinner?"

Jonah shrugged, relieved. "I think there might be more secrets here than you would expect."

"I suppose we'll find all the things you say you've seen at the Central Facility Computer, right?"

Jonah traced the lines of her sarcastic expression with his eyes, his heart beating slightly faster.

"I don't know what we'll find there," he replied.

"And what about your family?" she continued. "I remember that you said you had a brother *and* a sister – *three* children."

"Yeah, Lillian and Harrison."

"How does that work?"

"I don't really understand what you're asking," Jonah said, perplexed. "Why can your families have only two children?"

"Well – it's the only way it makes sense," she started. "If a man and woman have two children, then they basically replace themselves in the younger population. If they were to have more, then there wouldn't be enough room in the Facility for them. Eventually, we'd run out of resources."

"Then that's how it works," Jonah said. "The surface isn't like that. There's more than enough room, and more than enough resources."

Talitha narrowed her eyes and stared at him, leaning her head slightly to the side.

"Sometimes it sounds like you're just making up some fake utopia," she said. "Like you've researched how it was on the surface, and are just pandering to everything I've hoped for."

"Sometimes?" he asked. "What about the rest of the time?"

Talitha paused, biting her lip.

"The rest of the time, I'm just trying to remind myself that it's too good to be true."

CHAPTER EIGHT

The area around the Central Facility Computer was much less exciting than Jonah anticipated. It looked almost exactly like everywhere else in the Facility, except for an authoritative seal placed every few feet. The circular seal was of an odd looking white-headed bird, with a black square between its outstretched red wings. Between its open beak it clutched an eye.

He assumed, based on everything that Talitha had told him on the Magnet Tram, that there would be a tremendous amount of officers. However, he saw even fewer people than in the halls of the Coomy's Family Unit. Still, he stayed on edge. She also told him that only Regulation Committee Officers were supposed to have access to the Central Facility

Computer, which worried him.

"Through here," Talitha said just above a whisper, pulling Jonah through a door.

The room they entered was the largest expanse he had seen in the underground tunnels. Its ceiling was at least the height of two homes, and its length was at least sixty paces. The walls were abuzz with letters and numbers streaming in all directions – but the majority were scenes of hallways, dining rooms, Magnet Tram carts, and even washrooms. The people in the pictures went about their tasks, completely oblivious to the fact that they were being watched. In equal distance, the Sector numbers were written across the top of the walls.

"Wait," Jonah whispered, his eyes wide. "Do you mean that someone is watching everything that's going on in the Facility?"

"Of course," Talitha answered calmly. "How else would we be safe?"

"But... That means that... Wouldn't they be watching us?"

"Don't worry," Talitha said as she gently put her hand on Jonah's chest. "My dad worked here when I was younger. He said that no one watches anything unless there's an alert or a *reason*. The rest of the time, he said that they would just play games on their eyetiles."

Jonah's heart sped up – not from fear, but from Talitha's touch. She slowly slid her hand from his chest into his hand, clutching it. He struggled to catch his breath.

"Don't worry," she whispered softly again.

She walked – dragging him slightly – toward the center of the room, where there sat a single large padded chair.

"My dad said that everyone on the Regulation Committee has this as their assignment shift for at least a year, in order for them to be able to understand why the Regulations are necessary.   But most of the time, just like every other assignment in the Facility, the Computer is actually what is keeping things on track.   The only thing a person is really needed for here is to dispatch the Control Officers – though he's been part of a group that is trying to give the Computer complete access to everything.   So that buttons wouldn't need to be pushed by people anymore."

She climbed up in the chair, letting Jonah's hand go.

"Honestly," she continued, "it all seems a bit miserable to me.   I actually *want* to do something with my life...   Pushing a button when the Computer tells me to doesn't seem...   Well, like *life* at all."

Jonah gasped when she took a wire from the chair and plugged it into her wristile.

"Jonah," she assured, "I said not to worry.   Dad said that when he was here, one of his friends disabled the security regulator on the chair, so that the Computer stopped registering when people did or didn't show up to their assignment shifts.   When he did it, he accidentally disabled the access requirement, so that anyone can use it.   He was afraid of getting in trouble, so he never told anyone.   By the time that he was assigned back to our sector, Dad said that new workers were told by the Regulation Officers that it wasn't supposed to have an access requirement."

"Why did your dad tell you all of this stuff?" Jonah asked.

"Well – he wasn't really telling me...   He was telling my

mom, and I don't think he realized that I was old enough to understand. He actually tried working for the Complaint Committee for a long time, but requested to be transferred to the Regulation Committee after I was born. Most of the new workers are a lot younger than he was. I think he couldn't work for the Complaint Committee, because... Well, he complains too much. I think that's when I started getting unhappy with life in the Facility; when I found out that pretty much everything was pre-determined by the Computer and it didn't matter if I did something or didn't do something, but I'm sure his complaining didn't help."

She leaned back in the chair, which had obviously been altered to hold a larger person than was originally intended. She patted the seat next to her, urging him to sit beside her.

Jonah gulped. Even without anyone around to see him, he felt like his father's eyes were on him, testing him.

"Do you think it's... appropriate... for us to sit in the same chair?" he asked without thinking.

"Appropriate?" she responded. "Jonah – it's things like that that make me think you might actually be telling the truth... No one here would ever react like that, even as a joke."

She grabbed his hand and pulled him uncomfortably into the chair. He smiled nervously.

He watched Talitha scroll through various screens on her wristile, swiping at moving letters. She pressed on the screen, and the chair leaned back as the lights in the room dimmed. He couldn't help but focus on the fact that he was lying next to her, the skin on their fingers barely touching.

The ceiling faded into the scene that they had seen earlier.

A happy couple with bags walked towards an open door guarded by a uniformed man. Behind the couple was the same family of four as before, their toddler grabbing dirt. This time, he could hear sounds from the scene coming from the headrest of the chair.

"That's right, Bug," the father said happily. "You better play in the dirt a little bit longer, because you might not see it until you're a bit older."

The child's mother, holding an infant, laughed at both of them as the man stooped down to feel the dirt as well. "Come on, you two!" she giggled. "We don't want to hold up the folks behind us."

The man picked up his son and then the bags he had placed on the ground. The family then moved in through the door, followed by others.

Talitha sped up the scene briefly, then let it play out when a large red block with the word *Classified* overlaid the very top edge of the screen.

The scene seemed the same for a moment, until a loud crack was heard in the distance.

Jonah sat up, looking around the room, as did the people on the screen.

"It was on the screen, Jonah," Talitha said calmly, though she had also jumped at the sound.

"That was a gunshot," he said as he laid back down.

The scene on the ceiling grew more frantic. The families pushed toward the door quickly, and the guards snarled, "Everyone stay calm! If there is an emergency, we will be notified first!"

The families slowly calmed down and maintained their place in line silently. Moments later, a boxy vehicle drove up to the door and two uniformed men jumped out. The guards at the door raised their hands up to their forehead in a salute and stood straight, waiting as the men from the vehicle walked towards them.

"At ease, men," one of the uniformed men said. "We had a little trouble back there... Some narcissist was trying to smuggle in two unauthorized kids inside his luggage. The guy threw some punches and we had to terminate him. We let the kids go, but the guy's wife was flipping out. She ran off with the kids, so keep your eyes out for any possible targets."

"Sir, yes sir!" the door guards yelled.

Talitha and Jonah watched as the vehicle drove off and the scene played as if all was normal. Families continued inside the doors, children continued to laugh, and adults continued to smile and talk.

"What do they mean 'terminate him'?" Jonah asked.

Talitha paused before mumbling, "It can't mean what I think it means... I don't know."

After some time, Talitha touched her wristile to speed the video up and the people vanished. As one guard began to close the door, a woman and two children ran towards the entrance, screaming, "Please let us in!"

With no reservations, the guard reached for his gun and shot them, and then shut the door behind him as he entered the Facility.

Talitha's hand covered her open mouth, and she squeezed Jonah's arm with the other. He shook his head and tensed his jaw.

The scene was still; the three bodies silent in the middle of the screen. Talitha quickly tapped at her wristile.

Mr. Adams was visibly older in the next picture. His hair was completely white and his skin drooped around his eyes, even though he had put on weight since previous images. His voice was slow and quiet.

"This will be my last entry," Mr. Adams said, barely above a whisper, in the same book-filled room. "I would not call it a lecture as much as a confession, though one that I doubt will ever reach anyone who will care.

"In looking back, I'm afraid that I made the wrong decision. Like so many of us before the Surface's End, I was disillusioned. We, the Leaders, thought that we could destroy poverty, if only for a small subset of society. We set out to build the Facility, knowing that there would always be enemies, and there would always be needless death if people were left to their own devices. We were convinced that we could protect people from themselves.

"It started innocently. My predecessors had laid the groundwork of taking from the wealthiest of their time, and redistributing it to those with nothing. We, like they, thought that the poor simply did not have the same advantages of the rich. I did not see it at the time, but I'm afraid that in doing so, we sped the process of decay.

"Instead of things equaling out, it seemed that nothing was changing. The poor were still poor, and they continued to complain about the lack of opportunities. They quickly were no longer satisfied with the resources that we handed to them, and demanded more – which we continued to take from the rich who somehow remained rich. In recent years, I have realized that the more we regulated them, the more they simply figured out loopholes to remain as free to work and trade as they could.

"We built the Facility with the thought that we could create a society in a vacuum. At first we accepted volunteers – and there were a great many – from all over the economic spectrum. We tried to keep the underground citizens classless, so that everyone was truly equal. We soon understood that that could never be the case, as we could not lead if we were not Leaders, set apart from the rest. And then we realized that it took certain skills to maintain the Facility; some menial and some talented. Before long, we knew that we had created the same structure that was on the surface. The reason the most talented and skilled were worth more on the surface is because their rare results warranted it. The unskilled were worth less because their results were easily reproduced.

"Instead of creating a new, perfect society, we simply duplicated the one that already existed. But we couldn't admit that to ourselves, let alone the people we had spent so much time convincing. We continued to bring people in, thinking that we were on the verge of achieving our goals. Unfortunately, we angered many on the surface because of our selections of participants. Many of those that we selected to take part were found murdered shortly after they were announced, most likely because of jealousy. We started notifying people in secret, which caused its own problems.

"Before the Facility was completed, the government had

decided to move all operations into it, for fear that they would be exposed to attacks from citizens if they were to remain on the surface. Instead of a peaceful utopia, it was equipped with weaponry. Only a week or so after the doors were closed, citizens started attacking all entrances, and we voted to retaliate in order to maintain the safety of our people.

"In a horrible, disgusting vote behind closed doors, military leaders decided to launch several nuclear missiles that they had access to – not to decimate its own people, but to create an electro magnetic pulse that would destroy all electronic equipment within reasonable ranges of the Facility. Their reasoning was that it would stun the surface, and that it would drive everyone away from the site of the Facility to cities that still functioned normally.

"But something went wrong. We never knew exactly what happened – there were investigations and secret trials for years, and many people were imprisoned or executed because of their connections to it, but the details were never clear. Apparently far more missiles were launched than were intended, and they not only destroyed the surface of the country above us, but the entire planet's atmosphere. One theory was that it was a chain reaction; other countries started attacking once ours were launched. Either way, we knew that we couldn't go to the surface, and we couldn't let the citizens of the Facility know that it was our own fault.

"At first, I simply regarded it as a horrific tragedy. However, I have fought for the last few decades to have access to the recordings of the meetings surrounding this decision, but the current Leaders revoked my Facility permissions and prevented me from entering the Central Facility Computer.

"Now, I have become subject to one of the regulations that I helped create. Tomorrow is my one hundred and fifteenth birthday, and my stay of execution has been pushed as far back as it could be allowed. When we first implemented the birth limitations to keep our population under control, no one questioned us. Unfortunately, because of the Facility's technology, our citizens were beginning to live longer – much longer – than we would have on the surface. So even with the allowance of two children, when we saw the possibility of five generations alive at the same time, we realized that we had created another problem. Not only the limit of space, but also of resources. The Facility was built to draw resources from the surrounding land, and grow and raise food within its walls. However, as with living quarters, the space even for resources was not enough.

"We have found a temporary solution for some of the gathering of resources, by simply extending the reach of our harvesting machines when we are low. We have set Resource Officers up at each each sector section to monitor our usage and capacity – but I'm confident that it will one day prove to be insufficient. At least unless there are plans to create another Facility, but I'm afraid that our own actions have prevented that.

"As anyone who watched my first lectures could see, the problem now is not in the number of citizens, but the consumption of each citizen. Since the Facility maintains everything for us, there really isn't any purpose in our daily lives. As such, we consume more – both in terms of resources and entertainment. The labor class that we instituted for necessary tasks have become a stench to the general public. But strangely enough, I've envied them for years. With their actions, they have purpose. I'm reminded of a scripture when I think of them... *Sweet is the sleep of a laborer, whether he eats little or much, but the full stomach of the rich will not let him sleep.* I did not understand how that could be true when I was still on the surface, but ever since my idle stomach has remained always full, I have. And interestingly, the book that those words are from will no doubt be burned when they discover it under my pillow after the death handed to me tomorrow morning.

"To balance the creation of new resources, we knew we had to lower consumption. When we set an age limitation of one hundred and twenty years, very few citizens objected. I think they understood how much more they had already been given... If they were not in the Facility's care, that would have been a difficult age to reach anyhow, and they were happy to sacrifice themselves for the greater good. After all, the premise of this Facility was to allow for an equal opportunity for all, and they had already had their opportunities.

"Over the coming years, the age limitation crept to where it currently is – eighty years – with exemptions for anyone the Regulation Committee felt deserved it. It's quite interesting to allow my fate to be in the hands of children that were born in the very Facility that I helped create, but I suppose that it's justice. For the first fifty years in here, I was part of many of these decisions; deciding who lives, who dies. Deciding who had special favor in the supposed equality that we had forced upon our citizens.

"I was hailed as a visionary when we shut the doors. Some called me a savior. But I was stupid. At twenty five, I was only a child, and my childish ideas were all theories. I was far too stubborn to see that I had not experienced the world. Instead, I sought to convince men and women – who *had* experienced – that we could succeed where others had failed. I rose quickly in the political system of the time, and was given too much power.

"What a grand experiment we had planned. But to many of those above me who were siphoning the money and resources, it was more than an experiment. It was a guarantee that they would never have to answer for their actions. A clean slate, where they could control truth. I was unaware, and because I was proud, I was easy to manipulate.

"I've known the truth for a great many years now, but I've been a coward. They have paraded me around to infer that I approve of the new regulations, to show that the only one remaining of the original Leaders commends their activities. In return, they grant me a longer life.

"Or rather I should say that they don't kill me.

"I now know that the others that I started with have been dead for years. Not because of their *lack* of vision, but rather because of it. They could not stand by and watch this failed experiment silently, so they were silenced. All while the children of the old political system became the players in the new.

"Well, I can no longer live with myself. I finally, without reservation, have decided that an honest death is better than a deceitful life. I'm quite ashamed that it has taken me this long. I regret that I've waited until there is really nothing I can do to right my wrongs. They took away my access to the Central Facility Computer many years ago so that I could not alter my previous lectures, and everything I've recorded since is classified. My hope is that someone will eventually find my messages, and it will confirm what they most likely already know to be true.

"So, with that, I will suck down one last meal of Food Substance, which consists of what even I no longer know. I will spend one more evening with the stars, the ones I remember as a child, painted on my bedroom ceiling. I will read my illegal bible one last night. I know that God has forgiven me, and I am completely undeserving of that. But I hope that mankind will forgive me. Or at least forget me."

Mr. Adams pushed a button on a bracelet - smaller than the wristles worn by the current population - and the screen went blank. Talitha stared into the black ceiling, her lips trying to form words, but never speaking.

Jonah finally broke the silence.

"So - do you believe me now?" he said.

Talitha furrowed her brow and thought for a moment. "Well," she responded, "everything he said is horrible… But he still said that the Surface's End is real, even if the reasons were lies."

Jonah shook his head. "Don't you see?" He pointed to the blank screen.

"If the people in the Facility have been told lies all this time, why would he have a full grasp of the truth? Maybe something did happen on the surface. That would explain the metal I still find out in the woods, and why Schultz has a fire bulb like you have down here."

Talitha curiously mouthed the words *fire bulb* before touching her wristile again. "Maybe we can see the meeting with the military leaders he mentioned."

The screen once again lit up, with men and women dressed in silver uniforms decorated with medals and pins sitting around a large table.

"The people are getting out of hand," one of them spoke. "On the surface, of course. If we don't do something, this place will be a crater soon. But they're out of hand down here, as well. It has come to our attention that some of the population, especially the laborers, have been organizing to 'escape' from the Facility."

"Lazy traitors," another mumbled angrily. "There isn't a single one of those stupid rednecks that could survive without us. They don't have a clue what kind of opportunity we've given them."

"That's the problem, Barry," a woman's voice chimed in. "While they were on the surface, most of them didn't have to work and the government still paid all their bills. They're claiming this is some sort of prison. I don't know why Adams insisted we be diverse in our population."

"It's because he actually believes the cause he's preaching, Carla," the first voice said. "He really thinks that at some point, everybody is going to be equal. I can't wait until we automate their jobs so we can toss them back outside."

"That's going to take years - decades, maybe," Barry said

angrily. "We can't allow some sort of mutiny because these idiots want greener grass. As much as I hate them, we need them."

"There's a plan to add trace amounts of tranquilizers to the Chemvapor that is so popular," Carla offered. "That should quell their uprising but allow them to continue to work."

"It's a good long term plan," the first voice confirmed, "but it could also take years to take full effect. We're getting resistance from some of the Wellness Committee, saying it could have long term side effects."

"Long term side effects?" Barry yelled, fuming. "The long term side effect is that this whole facility could collapse on top of us in a week if we don't do something!"

"I know, Barry, I know," the first voice said calmly. "But that isn't how they look at things - like Adams, most of them have lofty ideals that aren't affected much by reality. We have an immediate problem, and we need an immediate solution."

Several of the younger attendees were fidgeting, obviously not comfortable with the direction the meeting was going.

"I tell you what will put them in their place," Barry laughed. "Let's take away their precious surface. Let them know the only other option is dead grass. It's going to happen one of these days anyhow. There are thirty different countries that we owe money to that are bound to drop a bomb on us any day now. And that would be a smooth way to get rid of those greedy pigs in Texas."

There was a pause.

"Sir?" a woman in her twenties said sheepishly. "You're not talking about killing innocent citizens, are you?"

Barry shot an icy look at her.

"Have you ever seen a war, little girl?" He leaned his head forward as he spoke, so that there was no doubt that he was talking down to her. She nervously looked down at a glowing tablet in her hands. "There's no such thing as an innocent in war. There's the enemy, and there's the potential enemy. If you turn your back on some '*innocent*,' they won't hesitate to take a shot at you."

"Nobody's talking about genocide, Barry," Carla tried to recover. "The Facility was created to *save* lives, not take them. General Hiller?"

The first man that spoke took a deep breath. "Carla, you know the old ranks are no longer recognized."

"Old habits, sir."

Hiller leaned back in his chair and stroked his chin. "Barry - I'm not fond of the methods, but you make a great point. We'd absolutely be justified to launch some missiles, considering the citizen attacks on military territory. And if there were no surface for the laborers to go to, they'd be easier to pacify."

The silence was heavy. Many of the attendees exchanged desperate glances, hoping that someone would declare that the possibility was unreasonable. When no one spoke, the glances grew more frantic.

"What if we faked it, sir?" a new voice chimed in hastily.

"Faked it, Stinson? I'm listening."

Barry's eyebrows furrowed, obviously not satisfied with a fake war, but everyone else looked interested.

"Yes sir," Stinson straightened up now that the whole room

was looking at him. "We could send a few missiles out to desolate cities - places like San Francisco and Minneapolis where the economies have been dead for years, and are almost completely unpopulated. You could even send one to Houston, Barry, to send the Texans a message."

Barry's face remained cold, but he nodded.

"We destroy already dead cities and show recordings to the citizens of the Facility. We could even detonate nukes a few miles above the surrounding area of the Facility to create EMPs. That would wipe out the tech in the surrounding areas, and the entire Facility is hardened against it. They'd leave fairly quickly because food and power would be hundreds of miles away."

"Interesting," Hiller said. "The only idiots that would stick around after something like that would be the religious nut jobs that have been living in the woods - people who don't need a power grid to get through the winter. And *they* wouldn't care to come around here to damage the entrances."

"But not only would we lose the vandals," the young man continued, "we could show footage from the surface - mostly from the decimated cities, but also of the abandoned entrances - so that it would be real to them. No one would be tempted to 'escape' to the surface if they thought radiation was waiting for them there."

"I like it," confirmed Hiller. "Anybody have any objections - or a better idea?"

The room was quiet.

"All right. Stinson, get me a list of cities that would be considered already deserted."

"Yes, sir."

"And Barry. Get me a list of locations that are an immediate danger. There's no reason that we can't neutralize some of the threats while we're at it."

The screen went blank.

Talitha sat completely still, eyes still fixed on the scene. Jonah looked at her face in the glow of the dim room, hoping that it was now obvious to her. He slipped his hand into hers.

"Do you believe me now?" he asked.

After a pause, Talitha quickly took her hand away from his and started touching her wristile. Jonah's cheeks flushed red, embarrassed because he thought that he'd crossed a line.

"I've got to tell my dad," she said, frantically moving her fingers along the glass. "Everybody has to know that they've been lying to us. For hundreds of years, they've been lying to us."

Jonah tried to shift his weight away from hers for fear that she was angry at him. "What makes you think they'd listen?" he asked, slightly detached. "You didn't believe me when I told you."

"I know, Jonah," she said as she grabbed his hand, noticing him inching away. She tried to pull him closer. "I'm sorry. I'm sorry I didn't believe you."

Her eyes pierced into his. "But I'm downloading these videos to my wristile so they don't have to believe *me*. So they can see it for themselves."

Jonah sat up quickly. "You're taking the pictures out of here? Won't someone know that they're missing?"

She sat up and put her hand softly on his back. "No, I'm

not taking them away, I'm just making a copy. No one will know that I'm taking it, because the original records are still on here."

Jonah looked around the room at all of the blinking lights and glass screens. "I don't think I'll ever understand how any of this stuff works," he said.

"You don't have to," she replied with a half smile. "We won't need it on the surface, right?"

Jonah's eyes shot to her face. "You're coming with me?"

"Of course I am!" she said. "My entire life, I've hoped that there was something else besides this horrible Facility. I've watched fake sunsets and smelled fake flowers. I've lived thinking that the only other option to a purposeless life was a radioactive death. You have rescued me, Jonah. You've rescued all of us!"

She threw her arms around him, getting him tangled in the cord connected to her wristile. Jonah knew she had said everyone, but he focused on the fact that she said he rescued *her*. They embraced long enough that he knew it was not just for celebration.

A three note chime from her wristile caused her to let him go and pull out the connected cord. As soon as the cord was loose, the lights in the room grew slightly brighter and the chair raised up around them.

She stood, pulling him up beside her, and kept his hand in hers. Jonah could barely breathe.

"Well, what are we waiting for?" he said. "Let's go tell them!"

She smiled and briskly moved toward the entrance of the

gigantic room, slightly dragging him behind.

.- .-- .- -.- .

Jonah and Talitha sat in the Magnet Tram cube, her giggling with talk about the surface. She unleashed countless questions, now that she was no longer afraid it was all a trick. To Jonah, her face - which held a sadness before - lit up in a way that made him even more intrigued by her.

Their hands were intertwined, the fabric on their shoulders pressed together. Jonah's heart raced watching her lips form words like a melody. He knew that this was the moment he needed to risk.

"Talitha." Jonah interrupted her. "I've never met anyone like you."

She smiled, exposing every single one of her teeth. "Well, I think that's obvious, Jonah," she laughed. "You're definitely the first person from the surface I've met!"

"That's not what I mean," he answered. "I'm... I'm very interested in you."

She gave an embarrassed smile and her cheeks flushed as she looked away for a moment. She put her free hand over his. "You don't have to say anything, Jonah. I'm interested in you as well."

"No, I do have to say it," he said. "I don't want to wonder if you know how I feel, or if I really know how you feel... I guess I'm trying to say... Can I court you? I know, I haven't talked to your father to ask his permission so this is not the way I should do this, but I just felt like I had to ask now."

Talitha's smile turned into a look of confusion.

"I have no idea what you're asking," she said.

Jonah's voice grew a little more nervous. "I'd like to court you... Pursue you..."

"The traditions of the surface must be very strange," she smirked. "Do you mean have a more serious relationship?"

"Well, yes," he replied, "but more than that. I'm asking if it's okay if I can pursue your hand in marriage."

Talitha's eyes got wide.

"This seems a bit sudden, Jonah," she said. "I'm only sixteen... We don't usually get married until we're thirty or so. Getting married too early seems really impatient."

Jonah looked down, defeated. "Oh," he said. His hand, held in both of hers, relaxed uncomfortably.

"But -" Talitha tried to recover. "I really like you, and I've never felt about anyone the way I do about you. I've never felt like anyone understood me, and it seems like you've been inside my head since I met you. It's not that I'm hesitant because I'm unsure of you. I'm just hesitant because I've never heard of this before. I really like you."

She put one of her hands on his cheek, raising his face so their eyes could meet. "Can I think about it?" she asked.

"Yes, you can take as much time as you want," he said, still a bit defeated. He didn't know what to think of the situation - the couples in his town would have never sat so close or held each other's hands without a formal courtship. He felt a bit embarrassed that he had assumed so much. "I'll even wait until the surface stops burning," he grinned.

"Well, I guess that means you're not planning on waiting very long," she laughed as the cube's door opened.

When they stepped out, instead of the usual line of people waiting to step into their tram cube, there was an empty room. Talitha and Jonah caught each other's glance for a nervous moment.

"Something isn't right," she whispered. "The Magnet Tram line is almost always full, even in the middle of the night. Our sector must be on lock down, or something."

They slowly crossed the floor to the closed door, which remained closed as they approached. Talitha furrowed her brow, and waved her wristile near the wall, but nothing happened. She started grazing her fingers across the glass on her wrist, obviously trying to open the door.

There were footsteps behind them. Turning, they saw four Control Officers forming a line in front of them.

"Talitha Coomy, you are hereby placed into the custody of the Regulation Committee for the crime of unregulated access to classified material and will be tried for treason."

Talitha looked at Jonah helplessly, then let go of his hand. She lowered her head and took one step forward.

"What are you doing?" Jonah frantically whispered.

Talitha didn't look up. "I'm complying with their order," she whispered. "They must have tracked us in there."

"No," Jonah whispered back, then raised his voice. "No!"

He grabbed her arm and ran along the wall, away from the Control Officers.

"Jonah - what are you doing? There's no way out of here!"

Talitha struggled to keep up, obviously not wanting to.

"I can't let them take you!" Jonah yelled as the Control Officers started running after them. Jonah and Talitha had a head start, because the officers were obviously surprised that they ran. Jonah had no doubt that their usual suspects didn't resist, and they weren't accustomed to using their training.

"They can track me no matter where I go in the Facility, Jonah! There's no use in running," she yelled at him.

"Then we'll just have to get out of the Facility."

Jonah grabbed a vent cover on the top of a wall, and pulled with all of his strength. The cover ripped off the wall after a moment, and he threw it at the oncoming men. Not waiting for Talitha's decision or permission, he grabbed her by the waist and tried to heave her into the open duct. Before he could, however, the officers grabbed her and pulled her down.

Two officers pulled Talitha to the side, while the two others clumsily tried to restrain Jonah. He punched the first officer in the opening in his helmet, forcing him back. He pulled his elbow back into the light body armor covering the ribcage of the second officer. When both officers stumbled back, he sprinted toward Talitha.

The officers holding Talitha shoved her to the ground and braced for the attack. He yelled out, "Get into that duct!" then he crouched and forced his shoulder into the stomach of the third officer, pushing him forward. Before he knocked him to the ground, the fourth officer wrapped his arms around Jonah's torso and wrestled him to the ground. As Jonah regained his bearings, the second officer was on top of him, punching him in the face.

"Jonah!" Talitha screamed, collapsed on the floor.

Between punches Jonah yelled, "Get to the vent!" Punch. "Find a way to the surface!" Punch. "Follow the flags!"

The third officer rushed in and started kicking Jonah in the face, causing blood to spurt out his nose.

Jonah saw the first officer's bloodied face approach slowly. Pulling out a long black stick, the officer touched the end to Jonah's forearm and the other officers immediately ceased their attack. Bloodied and exhausted, Jonah breathed out, "On the surface, find the Whitfields."

The first Control Officer wiped blood from his mouth and pushed the handle of the stick. "I never thought I'd get to use this thing," the officer said just before Jonah's body convulsed, arching up from the ground.

"I didn't request to be a Control Officer for this," one of the officers said as he pulled Talitha from the ground. "What in the world did he think he was doing?"

Talitha was crying.

"I don't know, but he's still moving," another officer said.

The first officer pushed the button on the stick and held it. "Guess he needs more than the recommended dose."

Pain shot through Jonah's clenched body as it convulsed out of his control. He couldn't hear his own screams above the hum of the stick's power in his head.

He slumped to the ground like a rag doll when he fell unconscious.

CHAPTER NINE

Talitha sat in the corner of her bright cell in the fetal position, rocking slightly back and forth. Her uniform had been changed to all black, and her wristile was gone. The walls of the room were uncharacteristically dull metal, unlike most other rooms in the Facility, which had interactive glass on almost every surface. This room looked a bit more like a Resource Duct. For the first time in her life, Talitha felt dirty.

Her father's hands gripped tightly around the bars that made up the door, white with angry pressure.

"What were you thinking?," he demanded. "You might have gotten me thrown off the Regulation Committee! Imagine a committee member whose daughter doesn't even follow regulations. Unheard of!"

Talitha continued to rock without looking up or responding.

"What did you even copy, anyhow? It's bad enough that you *viewed* anything on the Central Facility Computer, but to *copy* something from it... Are you insane? What could be so important that you would need to copy it?"

Silence.

"You heard that boy died, right? Stupid kid. Why in the world would he have defied the Control Officers - especially when they weren't even after him. Yours was the only unauthorized Identification Chip found anywhere near the computer. What in the name of the Leaders did he think he was doing to help you? And why *would* he want to help you, when you had just broken several regulations? Your mother said there was something strange about him, but this is unbelievable. I just got over the sickness, and now you're trying to kill me with stress."

Talitha had stopped rocking. "He's dead?," she asked, looking down, tears falling from her cheeks.

"Yes, he's dead. They can't even notify his family, I'm told, because his Identification Chip shorted out during his attack. And you shouldn't be worrying about him, anyways - you should be worried about yourself. Or at least your family, for Forefathers' sake."

Talitha's sobs grew louder.

"What did I do wrong with you?," Quilen wondered aloud. "I mean, Dawkin isn't perfect, but I don't think he'd ever pull a stunt like this. I should've put a stop to all of your dreaming and talk of the surface a long time ago. I wanted you to be happier, but I didn't think it would drive you to become a treasonous criminal. I'm doing everything I can to keep them from casting you out onto the surface, but I'm having a hard time."

"Let them send me to the surface," Talitha said, wiping her wet face. "Not that that's what they actually do. They probably just kill me and recycle me for Food Substance."

"That's hideous, Talitha," her father snapped. "You and I both know that Food Substance is synthetics. Or are you wanting to die? Should I stop fighting for you? Because if you don't even *want* to get out of here, then why am I putting my neck on the line? It'd be a lot easier for us if I could tell them to do what they want with you - that way they'd know that at least *some* members of this family are loyal."

Talitha drew a sucking breath of air through her nose. "What did they do with him?"

Quilen looked at her with astonishment. "What did they do with him? That's all you want to know? About a dead boy's body? Not 'how's my poor mother' or 'is Dawkin okay' or any concern about us? I don't know what they did with him. All I know is what they posted on the Public Messages; that *two criminals* - you're one of them, thank the Forefathers they didn't release your name - were apprehended, and that one of them died after almost murdering four Control Officers. They've been showing loops of video of him trying to kill them for the last twenty-four hours, and everybody's glued to their tiles even more than usual. You sure got the whole Facility in an uproar. We haven't had any attacks in the Facility for decades, so it's all anyone cares about right now. Some people have apparently been missing their assignment posts because they're watching it constantly. Not that they're giving much new information. They only said the bit about his Identification Chip not working because they're trying to find his family. They're hoping that someone with a missing son will come forward so they can end this matter. I told them that he's from Sector 20. Right? That's what your mother remembered. Said his name was Jonan or something."

"Jonah," Talitha corrected him.

"Jonah, then. I'll tell them to look for the records of a Jonah in Sector 20. Maybe if they can find evidence that he's the one that put you up to this, they'll go easy on you. I bet they'd be a lot nicer on you if you started telling them that's the case. That *is* the case, right?"

Talitha remained silent.

"Well, I hope whatever you found was worth sitting in this detention unit for possibly the rest of your life. Or worth *Jonah* dying. I'm going to go give them his name."

Talitha cried as her father left. She never felt that he was very protective of her in normal situations, usually telling her to be more normal and quit questioning things so much, but she never realized how little he cared. She had read books about men who fought for their families, and who sacrificed for other people rather than themselves, but she didn't know any of those men in the Facility.

Anyone but Jonah. And he wasn't even from the Facility.

Now that they had taken her wristile away, she had no proof to show anyone that the surface didn't really end. No one would believe anything she said now that the Regulation

Committee deemed her a criminal. She wondered if the Regulation Committee even knew about the surface - if anyone knew about the surface. Or if the lie had been passed down for so long that no one ever questioned it.

It would be hard to convince anyone on any committee, and they would probably just label her as a lunatic, influenced by some under-the-radar terrorist from Sector 20. Her face would be plastered all over the Facility Messages during her trial, if she even got a trial.

And this after she just discovered so much. About the surface, of course. But also about Jonah.

Not only was he constantly at risk simply being in the Facility, but he fought for her. Died for her. His last words were to give her the way out. The way to the surface - to her dream.

"I should have said yes," she cried out loud. He had put his heart in her hands and she asked for more time. She was caught up in what is common for citizens of the Facility to do, even though she shared almost nothing with any of the other citizens. Why would she share their views on love?

Why would she need another ten or fifteen years to know that this once-in-a-lifetime person, who she now knew loved her enough to die for her, was worth her 'yes.' She was afraid of a commitment, and he was afraid of nothing.

A 'yes' probably wouldn't have changed the outcome - the Control Officers would have still been outside the Magnet Tram, and Jonah still would've fought for her. But at least she wouldn't have to live with the painful regret. She would go the rest of her life - years, months, or possibly days - with a part of him that she felt like she didn't have now.

She climbed into the metal slab bed, covered her eyes to shield them from the bright lights that she could not control, and cried herself to sleep.

.- .-- .- -.- .

Talitha awoke the next morning when a metal plate of Food Substance flew through a slit in the barred door, skidding a few feet. The slop that once sat in separated piles made a trail marking the path of the plate.

"Morning, traitor," a Control Officer said, smiling. She noticed that he was missing a tooth, and his lip was swollen, and recognized him from the ambush. She diverted her eyes away from him and back to the mess of Food Substance as he walked out of sight.

She had a pain in the pit of her stomach that she'd never experienced before, and realized that she hadn't eaten since the previous morning. The pain had kept her up much of the night, and she assumed it was guilt, but when she saw the plate she knew it was hunger. The guilt was much worse than the hunger.

She crawled to the center of the room where the plate rested, and scooped globs of Food Substance into her mouth. She quickly consumed everything she could spoon up with her hands, and - stomach still growling - licked the plate clean. She stared at the edible smears on the ground, debating licking that up as well. In a Facility where excess was normal, they had given her less than half what she was used to eating in a single meal - which was far less than the others in her family.

Heavy footsteps echoed through the hallway outside, and she scurried back to the corner. She assumed it would be her father again, and she didn't want to look at his face. Her entire childhood seemed to have been a sham, and she would prefer not to be reminded of it anymore. She wondered if her mother would ever come to see her, or if the last memory she would have of anyone in her family was her father condemning her. He was never a man of affection, but surely her mother had compassion, or at the very least would have listened. But she didn't know.

She glanced up when a shadow crept into the room.

The footsteps belonged to a large balding man, tufts of graying brown hair combed to seem more substantial than it truly was. She recognized him from the times she was required to visit her father's office during the Purpose Assignment Committee's yearly assessments. All of the children would spend a day at the location of the purpose assignment they most likely would have - which was almost always determined by their parents' pedigree. Her lecture class was made up almost entirely of children of the Regulation Committee, so she would do what she could to get lost in the crowd so that her father wouldn't even know she was there.

"Do you know who I am, Talitha?," the man asked, breathing heavily.

Talitha put her head back down.

"I'm Mr. Gisk, the Chairman of the Regulation

Committee. Your father's superior."

It was obvious that he assumed she would be impressed, or afraid, or something. He was not pleased that he garnered no reaction from her.

"I only have a few questions for you today. Your father filled me in on an abundance of helpful information, and I simply need to fill a few holes."

Mr. Gisk snapped his fingers and a Control Officer brought a chair for him to sit on. He slowly sank into the cushion, not confident in it until it held his entire weight. Once he was completely seated, he took a deep breath, as if to rest. He then motioned for the nearby officers - whom Talitha couldn't see, but knew were always there - to leave the area.

"Keeping in mind that I already know much about you and your situation," he started cynically, "would you like to tell me *why* you and your friend Jonah stole from the Central Facility Computer?"

Talitha's mouth moved, but no words came out. She didn't know if the truth would help her or hurt her, even though she felt that what they saw and did was innocent enough. Obviously, she would expect some sort of punishment for watching videos on the Central Facility Computer, but her treatment told her that she had hit a nerve in the system.

Mr. Gisk reached into a pocket on his shirt, and threw the object he retrieved through the bars. It landed a few inches in front of her.

A piece of pecan.

"Your father was more than willing to let us overturn your

entire family unit to find clues as to what you would have been up to. It seemed that you didn't even try to hide this. Or the flowers. Were they supposed to be a message to us?"

Talitha looked up at him. "Message?," she asked.

"Don't play me for a fool, little girl!" Gisk yelled, red faced, and most likely would have stood up if it wouldn't have taken any effort. "We know the videos you copied. We know that you've been obsessed with the surface since you were a child."

She was confused. If they knew about the videos, and assumed the pecan had been a message...

"You know that the surface is safe?," she asked, bewildered.

Mr. Gisk laughed. "I don't think I'd call it safe, but the Leaders know everything, Talitha. Everything that has happened in the Facility before now, and everything that is currently happening here, is at our fingertips. It's unfortunate that your actions weren't discovered until *after* they took place - otherwise this might have ended differently. But you have simply exposed an obvious lack of security that we will now remedy. So, for that, I suppose I should thank you."

"My father knew the surface was safe, but let me be miserable for years?," she said, hanging her head.

"Oh, no, no, no," Mr. Gisk responded. "I said the *Leaders* know everything. Your father is far from being a Leader. Though, I now have more faith in his loyalty than ever with how he handled this situation."

At least her father hadn't betrayed her by keeping knowledge of the surface away for years - even if he betrayed her in every other way possible now.

"Your father, just like everyone here, has a part to play. He is told what he needs to know in order to do the tasks set before him by the Leaders. If he knew too much... If the Regulation Committee knew *why* they controlled the citizens as they do, then it would be easy for them to fail to do so. If the members of the Technology Maintenance Committee knew how the *entire* facility worked, rather than the individual machines to which they are assigned, then they would fail to follow our priorities. And so on and so forth with every committee."

Talitha barely heard what he was saying, focused only on one thought.

"You know about the surface... But you still allow the entire population to think that we're imprisoned here?," she cried.

"Imprisoned?," he said, looking genuinely hurt. "This Facility hinges on a delicate process. If one piece of the puzzle is removed, then our fragile ecosystem would collapse. Indeed, we're already on the brink of collapse now, but we are constantly making strides forward. I think we've finally figured out how to bypass the manual approval of the Resource Harvest Extension. I don't know why the Forefathers thought it necessary to require a Resource Officer to push a button to approve extending the reach of our harvesters. It is, on its own, perfectly capable of starting the action when supplies are low rather than sounding an alarm. But that's besides the point.

"If the entire population knew that they could go to the surface, almost all would stay. But do you know who would leave?"

Talitha thought of everyone she knew. She was the only person that ever seemed to want to leave the Facility. She was the only one that desired a purpose beyond the roles that the Facility Committees thought it necessary for her to play. Everyone she knew was content with moving through the halls and units, gorging themselves on Food Substance, tile games, and Chemvapor - none of which she'd ever acquired the taste for.

Except there was one group that she'd heard of, but never saw.

"The laborers?," she asked.

"The laborers," he replied.

"Talitha," he continued. "It takes a lot of effort to keep this machine running smoothly. There are many tasks that the normal citizen would simply refuse to do, and would in fact be disgusted by. These people never get to experience the life of comfort that the rest of us have, so they simply assume everyone in the Facility lives as they do. They are kept separate for a reason. If they even knew how *you* lived, let alone that there was a whole world separate from this place, it would be very difficult to keep them at their assignment shifts. You and I both know that if even half of the laborers left, then the machine would break."

She didn't know. The way everyone had talked about the laborers, they would be easy to replace if all of them magically disappeared. They were, after all, unfit for prestigious purpose assignments like the Regulation Committee. Talitha assumed that laborers simply weren't efficient at anything else, so they were relegated to menial work. But - what was efficient about the work that her father or his friends did?

"So, all I really need from you is to tell me how many

people know."

Talitha realized that his only concern was to contain a threat. If she and Jonah had told others, then word would still get out, even if both of them were dead.

"No one," she said coldly.

"I knew you would say that," Mr. Gisk laughed, "but I was hoping that you'd save me the trouble of having to question every citizen in this sector. Obviously, the laborers are the highest priority, but we'll get to everyone. If you tell me now, then your partners can spare their families the humiliation of trials."

Partners?

"Wouldn't you know if I'd talked to anyone about this? I thought you said you knew everything that went on in the Facility?"

"Yes, we thought the same thing," Mr. Gisk said. "But, we still can't figure out the true identity of your friend Jonah, and we assume you've figured out a way to bypass or mask the signals recorded by your wristiles. The one he was wearing had never even been synced with his Identification Chip. We usually can pinpoint recordings of conversations between two citizens based on when their two wristiles are in close proximity, but we don't know what wristile to track in your recordings. Previous to the decoy he was wearing, of course. And since it wasn't powered on, it still didn't help us.

"The only times we've listened in on your recorded conversations, it's obvious that you're both speaking in some sort of code. It doesn't pick up much of his speech. As if you were talking to an imaginary friend or a ghost. It wasn't until we listened to the recordings that we even knew he was at the Central Facility Computer with you. Without his wristile, we'll simply have to have some of our Control Officers listen to absolutely everything you've ever said. Very time consuming."

Talitha was amazed. Apparently the thing that all of the Facility citizens were reliant on was the very thing that betrayed their every word.

"Jonah was the only one I talked to about it. He was the only one who ever understood," Talitha sighed.

Mr. Gisk snorted a contained laugh, and then bellowed, "How sweet! Young love! Stupid, stupid love. It never steers you right. Did you manipulate him into everything - destroying his Identification Chip, dropping off the Facility's radar? Or did he manipulate you without telling you that he had already done that? Were his big blue eyes too much for you? I can give them to you if you'd want them."

"Shut up!," Talitha shot back. "Jonah didn't manipulate me! He was *from* the surface!"

"So you're saying you believed his story? Or you're just sticking to the plan that you both decided on?"

Mr. Gisk stroked his thick chin. "That's unfortunate... If you could've given me the new information I needed, I could've made the inevitable process easier for you and Jonah's other co-conspirators. But, dead men tell no tales, as they say, so you're my only option. The coming weeks will not be easy for you."

Mr. Gisk slowly stood, bracing himself on the arm of the chair and the bars on the door.

"If you remember something, or decide that you'd like to be shown a bit of mercy, I'll be listening," he said as he pointed around the walls and ceiling of the hall.

CHAPTER TEN

The next day, Jonah's body still lay lifeless on a mattress.

After he was declared dead, the Wellness Officers had tried to remove his Identification Chip to give to the Technology Maintenance Committee to see if they could determine his identity. While one Wellness Officer could not find a chip to pull out, he did find that Jonah had a heartbeat.

With the introduction of the Identification Chip, Wellness Officers were trained far less in actual medicine, and far more in simply reading the reports the chip generated. They had come to think of the chips as source of life - now implanted in the fetus even while the mother was pregnant - rather than an observation of it. If a chip showed no vital signs, the body was dead.

The only reason his body had not been disposed of is simply because the Wellness Officer had stubbornly asked for more time to try to find the chip, mostly because he wanted the recognition when he found it.

His colleagues marveled at a body not relying on a chip, and assumed that the chip had somehow disintegrated with the electrical black stick wielded by the Control Officer. They had no explanation for how, but they were not the kind of people to need explanations.

Jonah's body stirred while a Wellness Officer was reprogramming a machine that had incorrectly changed a bandage.

"Uggh… Where…," Jonah groggily spoke. "Where am… I…"

"You're in the Wellness and Pain Management Center, Jonah," she said smoothly, moving toward the door to press a large red button, and then returning to the machine. "Don't try to get up."

Against her wishes he tried to lift himself off the mattress, but found that he was strapped down at his wrists and ankles with bandages tied in juvenile knots. It wouldn't be difficult to tear free on a normal occasion, but at the moment he felt like he had lost a fight with a bull surrounded by honeybees. He noticed that one of his wrists was covered in bloody bandages, and had a glowing wristile clasped around it.

"You're the talk of the Facility, you know," the Wellness Officer continued. "The last terrorist we had years and years ago was taken down by just one Control Officer. It took four of them for you. I'd say that's impressive, but I wouldn't want you to feel like you did something good."

"…terrorist…?" Jonah breathed.

"Everybody still thinks you're dead. We're all fairly amazed that you survived, because your chip… Well, we don't know what happened to your old one, but it's gone. We added a new one, though, but it doesn't have all of your information. We know you're Jonah from Sector 20, but it doesn't sound like any of your family wants you back enough to go through the embarrassment of claiming a terrorist!" She laughed, her entire body shaking. "The three families that had someone with a similar name all denied that they knew you. Can't say I blame them. I'm Atria, by the way."

"…how do you know my name…?"

"That girl you were with when you attacked the Control Officers told us. I don't know her name - everyone on the Facility Messages is just calling her 'T.' I doubt we'll ever get to find out who she is. The only reason I know you is because I'm the only one that learned how to program the AMT4C in the lectures," she said, motioning toward the object she was working on. On the side of the machine he noticed the words *Automated Medical Technician (Version 4C)*.

"Between you and me, I'm drawing this job post out a bit, because I want to know why in the name of the Forefathers you would attack those young men. If I take back some information from the boy who is the talk of the Facility, well maybe *I'll* become the talk of the Facility!" She laughed again. "But in a good way, of course."

"…is she okay?," Jonah whispered, his eyes fully open.

"The girl? I have no idea. I know she was okay when the

whole thing happened three days ago," Atria snickered, "but who knows now! I don't think anyone would raise too many questions if a girl like her just disappeared out of a surface duct!"

"…Talitha…" Jonah closed his eyes, forgetting the pain in his body for a moment, focusing on his heart.

"Talitha, eh?," the Wellness Officer noted, triumphantly tapping her wristile. "Oh - I probably shouldn't say such things about your friend… I suppose even a terrorist might benefit from the statutes of the Diplomacy & Sensitivity Committee."

Atria turned her eyes back to her work, tapping on blinking glass on the machine.

"…am *I* okay?," Jonah asked.

"Well, that's a good question," she said. "I think the Control Officers weren't taking any chances after you attacked them. They hit you with a level six stun! I didn't think anyone could survive that. We don't get to experiment with that too often, since we're a peaceful people. Except for you, of course. But after we got the new Identification Chip in your arm, all of your reports looked fairly normal. You have plenty of bruises and burns from the Stunner, but I'd say you're lucky. Still, word is that you'll probably go out with the trash after you tell them what they want to know. But I probably shouldn't have told you that. Let's keep that between us."

Moments later, the door to the room opened, and Quilen Coomy entered. Out the doorway, Jonah could see six Control Officers with the black stick Stunners in hand. He had a feeling they would have them set higher than level six if they could. The door closed behind Talitha's father.

"Officer, I'd like to speak with the boy alone," Quilen said.

Atria smiled. "Sorry, friend, but if I don't keep working on this machine, the Wellness and Pain Management Committee will be calling on the Complaint Committee, who will probably tell the Purpose Assignment Committee to reassign me. I'm too old to learn something new."

Jonah glanced at her. She looked as if she might be around the same age as his parents - but it was hard to tell with the amount of makeup that covered her bloated face.

Quilen bitterly sighed, "Very well," and sat next to Jonah. Jonah got the feeling that it was a good thing Atria was in the room. Otherwise, it looked like Quilen would have added to his bruises. *Thank you, Lord, for how nosy she is,* he thought to himself.

"Jonah, you don't know me," Quilen began, "but I'm… very *close* to the girl you kidnapped." He looked at Atria, choosing his words carefully. Jonah realized that he had not met Talitha's father face to face, but only saw him through the slits in their dining room vent.

"Kidnapped?," Jonah asked.

"I'm here to collect information that would confirm that you coerced her to take from the Central Facility Computer certain— Well, what *did* you coerce her to take from the Central Facility Computer?"

Jonah pictured Talitha's face. He knew that if Atria was right, and his own fate was most likely sealed, he would have to answer very carefully to keep Talitha safe.

"It was my fault," he said after a moment.

"I know that," Quilen gruffed. "But we both know that the Regulation Committee - of which I am a part, mind you - will want a bit more information than that."

Jonah was deep in thought, trying to remember something from all the videos that he saw three days ago that would satisfy the question. He was afraid that simply telling them the truth - that he was from the surface - would put Talitha in more danger, since he doubted she would recant that she knew the surface did not end. It didn't seem that those in positions of power in the Facility wanted that kind of information to get out.

The machine Atria was prodding made a light chirp, and she cursed. Quilen looked at her across the room. "Something wrong?," he asked.

"Uh… Nothing bad, I just need to fix something," she responded, pressing buttons. To her dismay, the AMT4C moved to Jonah's arm and efficiently replaced the bandage that covered his stun burn. As it moved around his arm, Jonah noticed a sharp object in a small pouch of the machine near his fingers.

"It looks like you've fixed enough. The machine is working - please leave."

"Oh, but it's just going to take a minute to run another diagnostic," she whined.

"Officer!," Quilen yelled. A Control Officer entered timidly, holding his Stunner out in front of him.

Jonah grabbed the object before the machine retracted, while Quilen and the officer were preoccupied with Atria.

"Take this woman out of here - her job is complete."

Atria let out a loud sigh, and whined again. "But you were just getting to the good stuff! You've got me curious!"

Quilen's brow furrowed as the Control Officer sidestepped to her, never taking Jonah out of the direction of his Stunner. He grabbed her without looking, to which she responded, "Oh, all right - I'm going."

After they exited the room and the door shut behind them, Quilen grabbed Jonah's face with his hands with aggression. "You're ruining my life, you dirty little laborer!"

Jonah spoke muffled words through Quilen's fingers. "Don't you mean your daughter's life?"

Quilen shoved the back of Jonah's head into the mattress and stood up, letting go. "Are you trying to mock me, boy? You think you can come in and manipulate her by telling her lies? By giving her what she wants, however it is that you found out?"

"So, she told you?," Jonah asked.

"No, she didn't tell me, terrorist," Quilen shouted. "She's not even talking to me, and truth be told I don't want her to. If I never have to go back to the sector detention unit I'll be a happy man. She's ruined this family enough, not counting the years of her constant *dreams*," he said the word with disgust, "and never being satisfied. All we can do now is hope the Regulation Committee will keep her involvement quiet because of my position. The Chairman has allowed me to do everything I can to work into his good graces. We can just say she was killed in some accident so that we don't have to explain why she disappeared the same time as your little stunt."

Jonah was amazed. Anytime he had gotten into trouble,

his own father would dole out punishment, but would always embrace him with a tender forgiveness. There were countless times that he was afraid he'd simply gone too far, and that his father would never look at him again, but it never happened. No matter how much pain he caused his father, Thomas Whitfield loved him.

And Quilen Coomy now hated Talitha. Jonah was quite sure that Quilen didn't even know what his daughter had done, but was ready to crucify her in front of his peers. Just to protect his reputation.

"The chairman will see you in a few hours - he's a busy man, you know. But I requested to question you if you woke up when he was unavailable. If I can get something out of you, then maybe that will be all he needs to keep Talitha's involvement quiet."

"I'll only talk to Mr. Adams," Jonah said coldly.

"Who's Mr. Adams," snapped Quilen.

"From the... From the videos," Jonah said.

Quilen smirked silently for a moment, and then let out a laugh. "Mr. Adams from the children's lectures?"

"Yes."

Quilen shook his head, snickering. "Mr. Adams from the lectures, who has been dead for over three hundred years?"

Jonah had no idea how long ago the lectures had been recorded, but the lapsed time cleared the air. He considered the clothing and tablets of the people in the videos compared to the uniforms and tiles of the people he saw throughout the Facility now. It also shed light on why his town on the surface had little evidence of a previous civilization - three or four hundred years is plenty of time for structures to collapse and for nature to overtake them. And for its distant descendants to forget.

"Yes, Mr. Adams. I want to talk to him."

Quilen looked at Jonah differently than before - more like looking at a dog chasing its tail than a fox in a chicken coop. "You know that you can't talk to dead people, right?," Quilen asked, snickering.

Jonah hoped that that simply talking about Mr. Adams would buy him some time, since there wasn't much other knowledge that Quilen and he would share. If it led someone to Mr. Adams' last video, perhaps they would discover the truth for themselves. But for the moment, he was merely stalling.

"I think he has more to say, and I want to talk to him," Jonah said, not budging.

Quilen stared at Jonah in disbelief, and then started pacing around the room. He puffed hard on Chemvapor, the blue tube lighting up between his lips.

"You're telling me that my daughter got mixed up with a boy who thinks that he can talk to a man who has been dead for generations, and somehow convinced her to break into the most sophisticated security system in the history of humanity? Or are you just preparing to share a similar fate to his - much sooner than he did? I assumed that you had a gigantic traitorous plan, but could it be possible that you're just insane?"

"If you let me go back to the Facility's main video room, you can talk to him, too," Jonah said. "Will you ask the men outside if they would take me there? That's what I asked Talitha to do, but she didn't let me talk to him for very long."

"Yes, I suppose Talitha *would* listen to a lunatic like you, if you actually believed in your own fantasies."

Quilen walked toward the door, which opened.

"The Chairman of the Regulation Committee will be here soon enough. If you tell him what he needs to know, maybe the punishment he'll give you and Talitha will be swift."

As soon as the door closed behind him, Jonah moved the sharp object under his hand and patiently cut the strap at his wrist. He proceeded to cut the other straps tied to his wrist and ankles, and softly jumped off the bed. Talitha's father said he had hours before he would be interrogated again, but he knew that anyone could enter the room before that time.

He ran to the corner of the room, where he had spotted a vent near the top of the wall. He jumped on a table and – after some painful effort – pried the cover off with the metal object from the bandage machine. He weakly lifted himself into the vent, and crudely covered the vent behind him. He knew it wouldn't take them long to figure out that's where he went, but he hoped it would delay the officers a bit more than if he were to leave the hole wide open.

He crawled through the vent shaft long enough to know that he was at least a few rooms away from where he started, and realized that he had no idea where he was. The vent split off in multiple directions, and taking the wrong one would mean capture or simply taking too long to try to save Talitha.

He looked down at the steady glow of the wristile on his arm. He had no idea how to use it, but remembered watching

Talitha use hers with only the swipes of her finger. Touching a single lit circle close to his thumb, the wristile glowed brightly with new circles that appeared. Small images were centered in the circles, and below each was text. Reading and writing was never one of Jonah's strong suits, but he quietly sounded out the various options that were displayed: "*Facility Messages... Communication... Room Automation...*" The one that peaked his interest, however, was *Citizen Locator.*

He pressed the button, which took him to a different screen with the alphabet and a prompt of "Citizen:," and a blinking line. Hunting the keypad, he spelled out "Talatha." The screen turned red with an error message that read, "Citizen not found; please enter first and last name, or Identification Number."

He spelled out "Talatha Koomi."

The screen turned red again, this time displaying, "Citizen not found; did you mean *Talitha Coomy?*" Jonah whispered *yes* before realizing there were two boxes below for *yes* and *no.* He tapped *yes*, and after a loading message said "Searching..." for a moment, a blinking red dot appeared on a map of blue lines against a black background.

He whispered "*Yes!*" in celebration.

But he soon realized he had no idea where he was in relation to the blinking red dot. After frantically touching all around the red dot, he instead touched the small image of a house and ended up back at the main screen with the options and images. He followed the same steps to get back to the Talitha's red dot, and touched different images that spanned across the bottom of the map. When he tapped something that took him to a screen that did not look helpful, he tapped the home image and started over. He did this several times.

Finally, he touched the small image of a gear, much like the ones he'd seen at Schultz's. Boxes popped out from the side, which gave new promising options that he once again sounded out: *"Directions to Location... Save to Schedule... Schedule Magnet Tram..."*

He clicked *Directions to Location*, and like magic, the screen zoomed out, and shown a separate green dot, with a white line criss-crossing between the blue lines. It was obvious that these paths weren't through the vents.

.- .-- .- -.- .

After silently traveling through the vents for some time, Jonah was staring through the slits in the wall at a table. The white line directing him to the red dot lead him to this room, and he was looking at a wristile, plugged into a box on a table along the opposite wall. It was obviously Talitha's.

He looked around the empty room, hoping to find some clue as to where she was. When every nook and cranny had been analyzed, he slumped into the floor of the vent, defeated.

He had no idea what he could do, save trying to re-integrate into the Facility and ask questions. But he knew that previously he had the luxury of stealth - no one was looking for him, and no one had a reason to wonder about him. Now, he was sure that, as Atria had said, he was on everyone's mind. If he was seen by even a single citizen, it would most likely mean his - and Talitha's - death.

He closed his eyes, knowing that it was a miracle that he'd gotten even this far with the wristile. Searching through the options on the initial screen, he found nothing that could help him.

Instead, he slowed his breathing and listened.

At first, all he could hear was the air blowing against him, and the beating of his heart. But he relied on his experience hunting game. He had no rifle in his hand, but his heart and the wind were his constant companion. He tuned them out.

Against the metallic walls, he heard a faint noise. Like wind that was irregular, competing against the steady breeze in the vent. Stalking the noise, he slowly and silently made his way through the pathway.

As the noise grew louder, he knew it as the sound of crying.

When his eyes peered through the slits in the walls, he saw Talitha slumped in a corner, dirty and unkempt. But still the most beautiful thing he had ever seen.

"*Talitha*," he whispered, not wanting to be heard by any officers or trigger any recordings. She didn't respond.

"*Talitha!*," he whispered a bit louder. "*TALITHA!*"

She looked up, rubbing her eyes and nose. At first, she looked at the door, expecting one of the reoccurring visitors from previous days. When she saw no one there, she scanned the room.

"*Talitha*," Jonah whispered softly again, poking his pinky finger through the slit. "*Up here - in the vent.*"

"Jonah?" Her voice was frail and broken. She said it with

one part desperation, one part disbelief. She wondered if it was someone playing back his voice from a recording. But then she saw his finger.

She jumped up and exclaimed, "Jonah!," in a breathy cry, keeping her voice quiet. She ran to the wall, jumped on the metal slab bed, and touched his finger. "Is it really you?"

"*It's me,*" he said. "*Are you okay?*"

"They said you were dead!," she said, tears streaming down her cheeks.

"*Not yet - but close... Are you okay?*"

"I'm okay now that you're here."

"*I'm going to try to kick the vent open. Stand back.*"

Talitha stepped down from the bed, while Jonah turned himself around in the duct. He braced his back against one wall and kicked hard against the vent cover. Kick. Kick. *Kick.*

Finally, the vent broke free from all but one corner, barely held affixed to the wall by a single screw. Talitha subdued an involuntary celebration, but almost immediately jumped on the bed and pushed the vent closed.

"Someone's coming," she whispered. "Grab the cover and keep it closed."

With that, she quickly jumped off the bed and ran into the corner. Jonah barely connected into the lip of the vent, precariously holding it shut with the tips of his fingers. The edge dug into his skin, but he held tight.

A Control Officer stepped in front of the bar covered doorway, looking all around the room. His Stunner was extended in his hand. "What was that noise?," he demanded.

Talitha, heart pumping with excitement, jumped up and

kicked the metal plate in the middle of the floor toward the door. She passionately screamed, "I'm hungry, I'm dirty, and I'm tired! Why won't you turn off this light?!"

The Control Officer just smiled. "We were wondering when you'd crack. You lasted longer than I figured. Sounds like another day or two and you'll be happy to comply with anything the Chairman asks."

Talitha, figuring she'd need to keep up a fit of rage in order for them not to come back at the sound of new noises, jumped up and grabbed the two remaining slimy metal plates which had all been tossed into the middle of the floor in the mornings. She threw them at the officer, and they clanged loudly against the bars.

"Ha! Whoa, there, girl," the Control Officer snickered, "You're going to hurt yourself!" He laughed to himself as he walked away, sheathing the Stunner in his belt.

Talitha walked up to the door, making sure that the officer was gone, and ran back to the wall, jumping on the bed.

Jonah let go of the lip of the vent, slicing the skin of one of his fingers. He disregarded it, and rotated the vent on the remaining screw. He shot both of his hands through the opening to grab her in order to pull her inside.

Before he could, she put her hands on both sides of his face. And kissed him.

Electricity shot through his body, more powerful than the Control Officer's Stunner, making him feel like his heart was going to explode. The hair on his neck stood up, and goosebumps rose all over his skin. He grabbed her waist, and pulled her off the bed, closer to himself. Her lips pressed against his like they were magnetic, with a force that would never release.

She pulled away, her lips still barely grazing his. "And yes," she said adamantly.

"Yes, what?," Jonah asked, confused and floating.

"Yes to your question."

"My ques—"

"Yes to your question about pursuing me. I'll marry you today if I can."

Jonah, a huge smile crossing his face, bent forward to cross the tiny gap between their lips and kissed her again. Even though she had been trapped in the cell for three days, her breath was the sweetest thing he had tasted in his entire life. They remained embraced, him in the vent, and her lifted up pressing against the wall, for what seemed to Jonah like both forever and no time at all.

He lowered her to the metal slab for a second, took a deep breath, and said, "I have to get you out of here."

She held his face for a moment, then realized that they were wasting precious time. But it didn't matter to either of them in that moment. Even if they were caught, the scene felt perfect.

Talitha put her hands on the ledge of the vent entrance, and Jonah lifted her from under her arms. He rolled to the side as he lifted, until they both shared the cramped vent. It was everything he could do not to stop everything and kiss her again.

He turned back to the opening, and rotated the vent cover back to its original position, bent awkwardly. "*They'll definitely find it, but hopefully not immediately,*" he whispered.

They scurried into the depths of the duct, taking twists and turns away from the cell, and away from where he originally came.

"We've got to get out of this place," he said when they caught their breath with their backs against the wall. "We need to find Surface Duct 37(C)."

Their fingers were intertwined, and he didn't know if his palms were sweating because of their rushed movement, or because of how close she was nestled up against him. She raised his wristile, using his finger as a writing utensil. She quickly navigated to another map of blue lines against black, with a complex line between green and red dots. "Follow this line," she said.

They quickly but quietly passed through countless passageways, trying to guess which way to go when a hallway didn't exist in the ducts as it did below them. After a while, they could hear frantic footsteps filling the halls below them.

"I don't understand it, sir!" a Control Officer yelled below them. "All of the locators are tracking him, but when we enter the rooms, he's not there!"

"Keep looking!," another Control Officer snarled. "Check every cabinet and trash shoot. They can't hide from us forever."

"Could he be on a different level?," the first officer reasoned.

"The Central Facility Computer does not lie. If he was on a different level, it wouldn't be telling us that he's on this level!"

"Yes sir!"

The officers were tearing at everything in the rooms surrounding them, ripping down cabinets and breaking the glass in the walls.

Talitha looked through the slits in the wall after they had been traveling for some time, and recognized the surroundings, now occupied with multiple Control Officers tearing it apart.

"Jonah," she whispered a moment after crawling past. "Was that my room?"

"Yes," he said softly back, "that's good. That means we're getting close."

"Does that mean you could see me? Without me knowing?"

His face flushed red, embarrassed. "Uh...," he stammered, his stomach suddenly turning in knots, slowing down a bit. "Yes... I'm sorry - I didn't mean to—"

"No, it's okay," Talitha grinned sheepishly. "After everything you've done for me, I... It's okay."

Jonah apologized again, pausing mid crawl.

"Jonah - you can needlessly apologize later when you're finished rescuing me," she smirked, giving him a nudge.

A short crawl later, the duct widened out and they were able to stand. They passed by the fabric that Jonah had tied into the grates in the floor. He disregarded the wristile, making the rest of the turns by memory.

They stopped in front of the ladder, the same one that he found - *how long ago was it?* Jonah couldn't remember, but he pushed her up the rungs first.

"Wait, Jonah," she said suddenly.

"What? We're almost out!," he said desperately.

"I can't just leave, knowing what I know. Other people have to know that the surface is safe. There have to be other people like me - like the laborers - who don't want to be trapped down here. If we leave without telling them, the Leaders will just make up a story and no one will know the truth."

Jonah looked down the corridor, checking to see if there was any immediate danger. "What will it take to do what you need to do?" he said, after seeing none.

She let go of the ladder and found a panel in the wall labeled *CFC Terminal*. She grabbed a cable protruding from the uncovered opening and plugged it into Jonah's wristile. "*Uplink Established*" covered the surface, and she again used his finger like a paintbrush.

"Hopefully, my wristile is directly connected to the main terminal, because I can access it from yours if so. We're all given backup passwords in case one of our tiles has to be replaced, because then we can access a backup from the mainframe to restore on a new one. I don't need to get a backup, but with the same password I can basically use yours to control mine. Technically, I can access it if it's not directly connected, but it would take a lot longer," she explained as she tapped and dragged at the screen with his finger.

"I have no idea what you're talking about, but I'm glad you understand all this stuff," Jonah said, continuing to scan the area.

"I'm going to try to connect into my wristile, and send the videos out as private messages to…well… everyone I can," she said, trying to simplify.

"How long is it going to take?," he asked impatiently.

"I don't know yet - the files are large, but I should be able to initiate it without having to wait for it to actually transfer."

Jonah stopped paying attention, because he was focused on footsteps. He didn't know how close, but it sounded like the same floor grating that they were standing on. "How long now," he said, trying to remain calm. There were two sets of footsteps echoing through the chamber, moving quickly.

"It's displaying a progress bar. We're at twenty percent, so maybe another few minutes," she said, slightly shaking.

"Can we do this later?," he asked. "Can we come back in a few days and finish it?"

"I don't know, Jonah," she pleaded, "they might completely seal us out if we leave now. If they seal us out, then they cut off all chances of anyone else getting out. And if the Facility runs out of Resources, they'll be trapped until they starve to death."

"Ok," Jonah said, poised for the footsteps that were much closer. "But get ready for another fight."

Almost as soon as he said it, the two Control Officers rounded a corner and saw them. Their Stunners were extended, approaching quickly, but with caution.

"How much time now?," Jonah asked, stone cold.

"It's at eighty percent," she answered. "We don't have enough time."

He pulled the cable out of his wristile and freed up both hands, which resulted in "*Uplink Failure*" appearing on the screen. "Get far behind me," he sternly said to Talitha. She obeyed. She was afraid that trying to spread the message about the surface was not only going to get them both killed, but that the message wouldn't even get out anyways.

All of a sudden, both officers rushed toward them. Jonah easily kicked one of the officer's Stunners out of their hands, simply surprising the officer that held it. He then ducked under the other Stunner and rushed behind the officer, grabbing his arm as he passed.

He whipped the Stunner around, grazing the other officer, knocking him back only slightly. *They must have the power turned down*, Jonah thought to himself. He assumed they would only turn it up when they had him at their mercy, so that they wouldn't risk killing each other. The officer shook his head and stood straight.

Jonah was trying to wrestle the Stunner out of the officer's hands from behind him, knowing that it would be nearly impossible for the stick to connect with him without connecting to the officer as well. They struggled the Stunner back and forth, while the other Control Officer patiently moved behind them. As soon as he was at Jonah's back, he sprinted in and bear hugged him from behind.

The Control Officer still holding his Stunner yelled to the other, "Now hit him with your Stunner!"

The other officer, panting, screamed back, "He kicked it away from me - I don't have my Stunner anymore!"

"Why didn't you pick it back up?" the first officer exclaimed. "Where is it?!"

"Right here," Talitha said. She shoved the end of the stick into the officer at Jonah's back.

The power shot through all three of them, knocking all of

them down. The Control Officer at Jonah's back fell to the side, Jonah fell nearby, and the officer still holding his Stunner fell on top of it. The electricity surging through his body caused his hand to grip tightly around the handle, while his body convulsed.

Talitha turned to the other officer who was slowly standing, and adjusted the Stunner with her finger. She prodded the officer, and after a moment of spasms, he collapsed to the ground.

She ran over to Jonah after turning the Stunner off, and helped him up.

"Is he okay?," he asked.

"That one's just knocked out," she said motioning to the officer she had just taken down. "I heard they used level six on you - that was just level three. It's off now, though."

Jonah reached out to grab the Stunner from Talitha and walked over to the other Control Officer, still convulsing from the Stunner underneath him. He turned the officer over with the Stunner that Talitha had turned off, ceasing the connection to the officer's Stunner, and knocked it out of his hand. He first grabbed the handle of the black stick and gave it to Talitha. He then bent down and felt the officer's pulse - faint, but constant.

He walked over to the *CFC Terminal* panel and reconnected the cable.

"What are you doing?," Talitha asked. "Shouldn't we get out of here?"

"If I hear footsteps, this time we're leaving," he answered. "But since we're still here, we might as well try again."

She smiled at him and quickly stood beside him, using his finger on the wristile again.

"It's back at eighty percent," she said, continuing, "it must have saved the process, so it started where it left off when the uplink was reestablished."

A few tense, but uneventful, moments later, the screen said *Message Sent to 1,290 Contacts.* "I sent it to everyone from my Education Center - I figured that would get it into the public quick enough."

She pressed the wristile around his forearm on both ends, which released the clasp. The glass fell to the ground, uncovering the bandages that were wet with sweat and blood.

He nudged her up to the ladder, following behind her with both Stunners in one hand, dangling them as they both made their way up. Each rung was a small victory, with his body reminding him how much turmoil it had been put through.

CHAPTER ELEVEN

Standing over the opening to the Facility in the middle of a desolate wasteland, Talitha looked absolutely defeated. She was scanning the horizon all around her when Jonah closed the hatch, turning the wheel to lock it.

"This... This is it?," she asked with disappointment.

"No!" Jonah laughed. "We call this the Deathlands. I think this is what the Facility has been doing to the land, sucking all of the resources out of the ground for miles. No one comes out here."

Talitha continued to scan the cracked landscape, obviously *trying* to believe Jonah. Even if there was no fire and ash, the surface she dreamed of looked nothing like this. "Then why did you come out here?" she asked.

Jonah grabbed two apples from the cart behind his bicycle, still parked where he left it, and tossed one to Talitha. "I don't know," he said, looking toward the trail of flags that led out of the dry expanse. "I guess something just drew me in." He smiled as he took a bite.

Talitha turned the apple in her hands, studying it, smelling it. She cautiously took a small bite with surprised effort.

"Make sure you chew this time," Jonah chuckled.

"What is this?," Talitha belted as her eyes widened, taking a larger bite. The juice from the fruit dripped down her chin.

"An apple," Jonah said, amused that in moments previous, he was in a world in which everything was confusing to him. She had been fluent in every aspect of the Facility, but here she was a newborn, experiencing everything for the first time. Here, Jonah was the expert.

"I thought it looked like an apple," she said as she chewed, "but the taste! More than that - the *texture*! I've never... This is *nothing* like Food Substance!"

Jonah smiled as he readied his bike. He and Talitha were both sweating from the sun directly overhead, and Talitha's pale skin would burn soon, though she didn't know. She was closing her eyes, facing the bulb in the sky, with her arms wide at her sides, as if to soak as much of it in as possible.

"Let's get you into some shade," he said.

.- .-- .- -.- .

They followed the flags for what seemed like hours. They tried several options with the bike - both sitting on the small seat, Jonah on the Bike with Talitha in the trailer - but they decided it was better for his tattered body to slowly walk beside it than try to struggle to move it forward with both of their weight.

When they approached the final flag, the entire green landscape came into view. Talitha, having a hard time containing her excitement, broke out into a run toward Jonah's tree. She hesitated, deciding to wait for Jonah.

He simply smiled and said, "Go ahead."

She ran the rest of the way.

When Jonah finally crossed the threshold of dead grass - because the Facility's harvesters had been extended even further while they were below the surface - he found Talitha picking wildflowers and smelling them individually in deep breaths. She had already been dirty, but now she was covered in actual dirt, and she was thrilled.

She asked him, "What's this?," and "Does this grow on its own?," and countless other questions about each thing she touched. Jonah could only smile and tell her what he knew, though occasionally admitting, "I have no idea."

When they passed the tree, Jonah started answering questions about his family.

"I look terrible," Talitha said, self-consciously. "I need to sanitize myself before I meet them."

Jonah laughed. "You look beautiful," he said. "And don't worry - they're probably as dirty as we are."

She looked back for a moment just as the Deathlands faded from view.

The story continues with

THE DIRT
WALKERS

ACKNOWLEDGEMENTS

Thank you to Holly.

Thank you to my mom - the only reason I finished this book is because I sent her a version that was only half complete. She mentioned it often, wanting to know how it ended, which drove me to keep writing down the story I already saw in my head.

Thanks also to my dad, who showed me what it meant to work hard and follow through on the things that matter.

Thanks to all of my family, who have been incredibly supportive in everything I do.

Thanks to Jeff Brinkley, Jeff Hildebrand, Brad Lawrence, Matt Lawrence, and Andy Neale for their brotherhood in Manic Bloom, and for forcing me to grow creatively.

Thanks to Deborah T. Bickmore, Seth Ervin and Casey Eanes for sharing wisdom about the book-writing landscape. Take away the music that usually accompanies my written word, and my legs are a bit shaky.

Thanks to Michael Hutzel for making the cover of this book look way better than what I was planning on releasing. Thanks also to Kelly McClain for sharing her font wisdom.

Thanks to my beta readers for their feedback, corrections, critiques and encouragement:

Deborah T. Bickmore
Walter & Amy Campbell
Casey Eanes
Seth Ervin
Nancy Hasting
Jeff Hess
Matt & Kim Kinnamon
Eric Klumpe
Corey Maass
Elizabeth Shrum
Ann & Barney Stevenson
Holly W. Stevenson
Kevin & Nicole Stevenson

I owe my life to Jesus Christ, and I hope that everything I do - including this book - reflects my gratitude.

And, last but not least, thank YOU very much for reading this, and for any support you have given me. If you like this book, please tell your friends, share online, write a review, and buy copies to give to everyone you know. If you don't like it... Well, let's keep that between us.

ABOUT THE AUTHOR

David Joel Stevenson lives outside of Nashville, TN, and is possibly surrounded by several chickens and thousands of honey bees. He is the singer in the band Manic Bloom (www.ManicBloom.com), a songwriter, a computer programmer, and is irregularly documenting his quests in homesteading on his blog, www.GeekOffGrid.com.

For more information, visit www.DavidJoelStevenson.com

Made in the USA
Middletown, DE
22 February 2020